TREASURE HUNTERS

BOOKS BY JAMES PATTERSON
FOR YOUNG READERS

THE MIDDLE SCHOOL NOVELS

Middle School, The Worst Years of My Life
(with Chris Tebbetts, illustrated by Laura Park)

Middle School: Get Me out of Here!
(with Chris Tebbetts, illustrated by Laura Park)

Middle School: My Brother Is a Big, Fat Liar
(with Lisa Papademetriou, illustrated by Neil Swaab)

Middle School: How I Survived Bullies, Broccoli, and Snake Hill
(with Chris Tebbetts, illustrated by Laura Park)

THE I FUNNY NOVELS

I Funny
(with Chris Grabenstein, illustrated by Laura Park)

I Even Funnier
(with Chris Grabenstein, illustrated by Laura Park)

THE DANIEL X NOVELS

The Dangerous Days of Daniel X
(with Michael Ledwidge)

Watch the Skies
(with Ned Rust)

Demons and Druids
(with Adam Sadler)

Game Over
(with Ned Rust)

Armageddon
(with Chris Grabenstein)

OTHER ILLUSTRATED NOVELS

Treasure Hunters
(with Chris Grabenstein and Mark Shulman,
illustrated by Juliana Neufeld)

Daniel X: Alien Hunter
(graphic novel; with Leopoldo Gout)

Daniel X: The Manga, Vols. 1–3
(with SeungHui Kye)

*For previews of upcoming books in these series
and other information, visit www.MiddleSchoolBooks.com,
www.IFunnyBooks.com, and www.Daniel-X.com.*

*For more information about the author,
visit www.JamesPatterson.com.*

TREASURE HUNTERS

BY **JAMES PATTERSON**

AND **CHRIS GRABENSTEIN,**
WITH **MARK SHULMAN**

ILLUSTRATED BY
JULIANA NEUFELD

LITTLE, BROWN AND COMPANY
NEW YORK BOSTON

Copyright © 2013 by James Patterson
Illustrations by Juliana Neufeld

Little, Brown and Company

Hachette Book Group
237 Park Avenue, New York, NY 10017
Visit our website at www.lb-kids.com

Little, Brown and Company is a division of Hachette Book Group, Inc.
The Little, Brown name and logo are trademarks of Hachette Book Group, Inc.

The publisher is not responsible for websites (or their content) that are not owned by the publisher.

First Edition: September 2013
First International Edition: September 2013

Library of Congress Cataloging-in-Publication Data

Patterson, James, 1947–
Treasure hunters / by James Patterson, Chris Grabenstein, and Mark
Shulman ; [illustrations by Juliana Neufeld].—1st ed.
    p. cm.— ([Treasure hunters ; 1])
Summary: "Following clues left by their missing father, twelve-year-old
twins Bickford and Rebecca Kidd sail from the Caribbean to New York
City with their siblings to finish the dangerous quest of their world-famous
treasure-hunting parents"—Provided by publisher.
    ISBN 978-0-316-20756-0 (hc) / ISBN 978-0-316-24262-2 (int'l)
[1. Adventure and adventurers—Fiction. 2. Buried treasure—Fiction.
3. Seafaring life—Fiction. 4. Missing persons—Fiction. 5. Brothers and
sisters—Fiction. 6. Twins—Fiction. 7. New York (N.Y.)—Fiction.] I.
Grabenstein, Chris. II. Shulman, Mark, 1962– III. Neufeld, Juliana, 1982–
ill. IV. Title.
    PZ7.P27653Tre 2013
    [Fic]—dc23
                                                2012040968

10 9 8 7 6 5 4 3 2

RRD-C

Printed in the United States of America

For Owen Ellington Pietsch
—JP

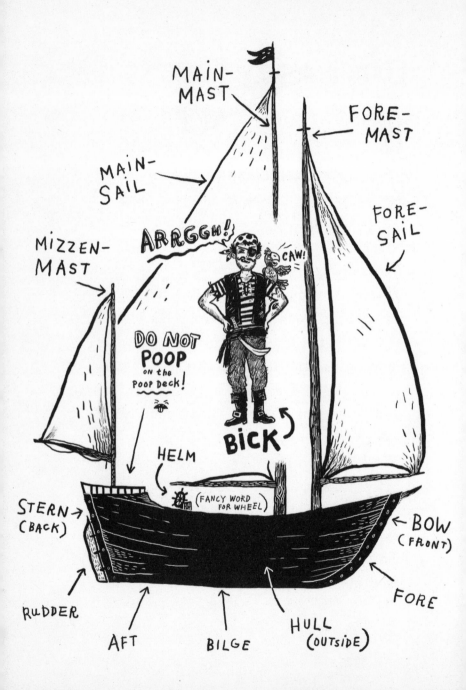

A Quick Note from Bick Kidd

Just so you know, I'm the one who'll be telling you this story, but my twin sister, Beck (who's wickedly talented and should go to art school or show her stuff in a museum or something), will be doing the drawings.

Like the one over there on the left.

I'm telling you this up front because, even though we're twins, Beck and I don't always see everything exactly the same way. For instance, I don't look like the way she drew me. I'm twelve. I don't have a mustache *or* an eye patch. So don't believe everything you see.

Fine. Beck says I have to tell you not to believe everything I say, either. Whatever. Can we get on with the story? Good.

Hang on tight.

Things are about to get hairy.

And wet. Very, very wet.

PROLOGUE

LOST
AT SEA

1

L et me tell you about the last time I saw my dad.

We were up on deck, rigging our ship to ride out what looked like a perfect storm.

Well, it was perfect if you were the storm. Not so much if you were the people being tossed around the deck like wet gym socks in a washing machine.

We had just finished taking down and tying off the sails so we could run on bare poles.

"Lash off the wheel!" my dad barked to my big brother, Tailspin Tommy. "Steer her leeward and lock it down!"

"On it!"

Tommy yanked the wheel hard and pointed our bow downwind. He looped a bungee cord through the wheel's wooden spokes to keep us headed in that direction.

"Now get below, boys. Batten down the hatches. Help your sisters man the pumps."

Tommy grabbed hold of whatever he could to steady himself and made his way down into the deckhouse cabin.

Just then, a monster wave lurched over the starboard side of the ship and swept me off my feet. I slid across the slick deck like a hockey puck on ice. I might've gone overboard if my dad hadn't reached down and grabbed me a half second before I became shark bait.

"Time to head downstairs, Bick!" my dad shouted in the raging storm as rain slashed across his face.

"No!" I shouted back. "I want to stay up here and help you."

"You can help me more by staying alive and not

letting *The Lost* go under. Now hurry! Get below."

"B-b-but—"

"Go!"

He gave me a gentle shove to propel me up the tilting deck. When I reached the deckhouse, I grabbed onto a handhold and swung myself around and through the door. Tommy had already headed down to the engine room to help with the bilge pumps.

Suddenly, a giant sledgehammer of salt water slammed into our starboard side and sent the ship tipping wildly to the left. I heard wood creaking. We tilted over so far I fell against the wall while our port side slapped the churning sea.

We were going to capsize. I could tell.

But *The Lost* righted itself instead, the ship tossing and bucking like a very angry beached whale.

I found the floor and shoved the deckhouse hatch shut. I had to press my body up against it. Waves kept pounding against the door. The water definitely wanted me to let it in.

That wasn't going to happen. Not on my watch.

I cranked the door's latch to bolt it tight.

I would, of course, reopen the door the instant my dad finished doing whatever else needed to be done up on deck and made his way aft to the cabin. But, for now, I had to stop *The Lost* from taking on any more water.

If that was even possible.

The sea kept churning. *The Lost* kept lurching. The storm kept sloshing seawater through every crack and crevice it could find.

Me? I started panicking. Because I had a sink-ing feeling (as in "We're gonna sink!") that this could be the end.

I was about to be drowned at sea.

Is twelve years old too young to die?

Apparently, the Caribbean Sea didn't think so.

2

I waited and waited, but my dad never made it aft to the deckhouse cabin door.

Through the forward windows, I could see waves crashing across our bobbing bow. I could see the sky growing even darker. I could see a life preserver rip free from its rope and fly off the ship like a doughnut-shaped Frisbee.

But I couldn't see Dad.

I suddenly realized that my socks were soaked with the seawater that was slopping across the floor. And I was up on the main deck.

"Beck?" I cried out. "Tommy? Storm?"

My sisters and brother were all down in the lower cabins and equipment rooms, where the water was undoubtedly deeper.

They were trapped down there!

I dashed down the four steep steps into the hull quarters as quickly as I could. The water was up to my ankles, then my knees, then my thighs,

and, finally, my waist. You ever try to run across the shallow end of a swimming pool? That's what I was up against. But I had to find my family.

Well, what was left of it.

I trudged from door to door, frantically searching for my siblings.

They weren't in the engine room, the galley,

or my parents' cabin. I knew they couldn't be in The Room, because its solid steel door was locked tight and it was totally off-limits to all of us.

I slogged my way forward as the ship kept rocking and rolling from side to side. Whatever wasn't nailed down was thumping around inside the cupboards and cabinets. I heard cans of food banging into plastic dishes that were knocking over clinking coffee mugs.

I started pounding on the walls in the narrow corridor with both fists. The water was up to my chest.

"Hey, you guys? Tommy, Beck, Storm! Where are you?"

No answer.

Of course my brother and sisters probably couldn't hear me, because the tropical storm outside was screaming even louder than I was.

Suddenly, up ahead, a door burst open.

Tommy, who was seventeen and had the kind of bulging muscles you only get from crewing on a sailing ship your whole life, had just put his shoulder to the wood to bash it open.

"Where's Dad?" he shouted.

"I don't know!" I shouted back.

That's when Beck and my big sister, Storm, trudged out of the cabin that was now their water-logged bedroom. A pair of 3-D glasses was floating on the surface of the water. Beck plucked them up and put them on. She'd been wearing them most of the time ever since our mom disappeared.

"Was Dad on a safety line?" asked Storm, sounding as scared and worried as I felt.

All I could do was shake my head.

Beck looked at me, and even though her 3-D glasses were shading her eyes, I could tell she was thinking the same thing I was. We're twins. It happens.

In our hearts, we both knew that Dad was gone.

Because anything up on deck that hadn't been tied down had been washed overboard by now.

From the sad expressions on their faces, I knew Storm and Tommy had figured it out, too. Maybe they'd been looking out a porthole when that life preserver went flying by.

Shivering slightly, we all moved together to form a close circle and hug one another tight.

The four of us were the only family we had left.

Tommy, who'd been living on boats longer than any of us, started mumbling an old sailor's prayer:

"Though Death waits off the bow, we'll not answer to him now."

I hoped he was right.

But I had a funny feeling that Death might not take no for an answer.

THE END

PART 1

PIRATE-INFESTED WATERS

CHAPTER 1

Whoa, not so fast.

You didn't really think that was The End, did you? If I were dead, how could I be telling you this story?

Okay. Fine. Beck says she could've taken over. That writing is easier than drawing. Whatever. Scribble a picture or something.

Note to self: If I ever have a ship of my own, do not call it *The Lost*. Because that's exactly what (and where) we were: lost at sea. I guess we should be glad Dad didn't name his boat *The Sunk*, *The Drowned*, or *Titanic II*.

When the storm finally calmed, the four of

us had, somehow, survived (for the moment, anyway). Yes, *The Lost* was still leaking, we all had seaweed in our shoes, and the ship-to-shore radio was dead. But *we* were all still alive.

Unfortunately, we couldn't say the same thing about Dad.

He was definitely missing. Gone. And none of us were sure what had happened to him.

"He went overboard," said Storm matter-of-factly. She's two years older than me and Beck, and she's such a genius (her IQ scores are off the charts) she's kind of socially awkward. She's always spouting stuff people don't really want to hear. "He's dead. Probably drowned."

"Hang on," I said. "We don't know that for certain."

Storm hesitated. "You're right. The sharks could've eaten him first."

I probably would've taken a swing at anyone else who said that. But it's just the way Storm is, and I knew she was as sad as the rest of us.

What made Dad's disappearance even more

depressing was the fact that just three months ago, our mother had disappeared, too. She went missing in Cyprus.

"Those shady dealers probably shot her" was what Storm had blurted out back then. "One of them had an Uzi submachine gun hidden under the left flap of his tan double-breasted trench coat. There were dried tzatziki dip stains on the lapels."

Did I mention that Storm has a photographic memory?

Long story short—without a mother or a father, Storm, Tommy, Beck, and I were now officially orphans drifting across the Caribbean Sea in our very own slowly sinking orphanage.

Of course, we weren't always this miserable.

Not to brag, but four months ago, we were probably the most incredible family anybody could ever meet. Not because of anything any of us did but because of who our dad was: Professor Tom Kidd.

That's right. *The* Tom Kidd.

The world-famous oceanographer and treasure hunter.

The guy who found the 1621 wreck of the Spanish galleon *Nuestra Señora del Mar de Oro* off the coast of Barbados (it was loaded with gold coins, bars of silver, and sacks of Colombian emeralds). In Asia, he uncovered thousands of pieces of ceramic pottery dating back to the Ming dynasty in the hold of a sunken cargo vessel. Off the coast of Cyprus, in the Mediterranean Sea, he brought up a treasure chest filled with sparkling jewels and diamond-encrusted religious artifacts.

And we were his crew. We were treasure hunters, too!

Our parents homeschooled us and taught us how to survive in the real world—without iPods, iPhones, iPads, or Papa John's Pizza. We're at least two grades beyond where we would be in a regular school.

(Well, maybe not Tailspin Tommy. He's seventeen and spends a lot of time on personal grooming, so he's probably somewhere around his regular grade level.)

I have never been to a mall.

Beck has never had a mani-pedi.

Tommy didn't need a gym membership at Bally Total Fitness to pump up his pecs.

And Storm can out-Google Google with our onboard computer because she remembers every web page she's ever surfed across.

Yep, ever since Beck and I were three, our home and our school have been this incredible,

PROBABLY LIKE, 500 YEARS OLD!

THATS WORTH APROXIMATELY $33,000.

sixty-three-foot-long sailing ship. This is where we learned to cook, took karate lessons (Dad has a black belt), and practiced navigating by the stars.

The Lost has taken us to more ports and countries than any of us can remember. (Except Storm, who, like I said, remembers everything— even what kind of food stains you have on your raincoat.)

Nine years later, it's totally normal for Beck and me to read a treasure map, go on deep-sea dives with our dad, and help him dredge up price-less Viking shields from an eleventh-century shipwreck in the Skuldelev Narrows in Denmark because a museum in Oslo is willing to pay top dollar to add them to its collection.

What *isn't* normal is throwing around a base-ball in a backyard. Grass feels funny under my feet. Plus, when you throw baseballs on a boat, you lose them.

The same way we kind of lost Dad.

Yeah, until Cyprus and, now, The Perfect

Storm, life on *The Lost* had always been extremely great.

Too bad our happy life was going to end when we sank and everybody drowned.

Unless, like Storm said, the sharks got us first.

CHAPTER 2

I think my parents nicknamed my big brother "Tailspin" Tommy because he usually has this seriously confused look on his face.

Unless he's navigating a ship.

Then the guy is like a laser. Completely focused.

As the day dragged on and the sun scorched away every single cloud in

TOMMY THE SEAHUNK

the sky, Tommy stood in the wheelhouse, squinting at his instruments and ignoring the blistering heat. This was hard to do. The deck was so hot my feet were sizzling like sausages on a grill.

"Are we totally lost?" I asked.

"Definitely." Tommy nudged the wheel a little to the left.

"Are you laying in a course?"

"Nah. I'm just goin' with the flow, bro."

"What?"

"The equatorial current. The Cayman Islands are directly in its path."

"So, we're basically drifting?"

"Basically. The GPS is dead. Didn't like being submerged in salt water."

Beck, who was still wearing those 3-D glasses, came up to join us.

"We're still taking on water," she reported. "Big-time."

Tommy nodded. He remained remarkably mellow, no matter how much bad news we hurled his way. "No worries. I'm only burning fuel to power the generators and, you know, keep the bilge pump batteries stoked."

Now Storm joined us outside the deck cabin. She was eating a Twinkie she must've found floating around down in the galley. The wrapper had kept the moist sponge cake from getting too soggy.

"We should have a funeral," she said.

Tommy got that tailspin look of confusion on his face. "For the dead GPS?"

"No. Dad. And Mom."

"They're not dead," I said.

"They might be," said Beck.

"Well, you don't have funerals for people who *might* be dead. You wait."

"For what?"

"I don't know. Maybe till you have a body to bury?"

Storm shook her head. "Not gonna happen. Sharks." To emphasize her point, she chomped off a chunk of her Twinkie.

So we decided to go ahead and have a funeral at sea.

Beck found Dad's favorite hat—this navy sweat-stained, beat-up old yachting cap sporting golden anchors on a golden life preserver. Dad has worn the captain's hat so much the sun and salt water had faded the gold to popcorn yellow.

Mom had bought the hat for Dad when he first started treasure hunting on his own boat.

We took turns holding the hat and remembering Dad and Mom.

Beck, who was technically the youngest (by two minutes), went first.

"Thanks for giving us the best birthday parties ever," she said. "And thank you especially for that incredibly awesome coconut pirate head from Hawaii."

That made me smile. On our birthday, Mom and Dad would always take Beck and me into the nearest port and let us pick out the coolest

presents ever. My favorite was the samurai sword
we'd found in Hong Kong. Instead of ice cream
and cake, we'd always have whatever exotic dessert the locals loved best. Sometimes the desserts
would be on fire, so we'd blow them out instead of
birthday candles.

I was up next.

"I remember the first time Mom and Dad took
Beck and me on a dive. Not the first time we put

on scuba gear, but the first time we went down to a real shipwreck. We both found these incredibly cool old Roman coins. Later I asked Dad if he had planted the coins so Beck and I could find them."

"Did he?" asked Beck, who'd probably wondered the same thing.

I shook my head. "Nope. He said the sea would never go easy on us, so neither would he and neither would Mom. We found those coins fair and square. We were officially treasure hunters. Thanks, Dad. Thanks for teaching us we could handle anything the ocean or life threw at us."

"Except this," said Storm, opening up her arms to take in the ship, the sea, and the enormity of our generally sucky situation.

We all stared at her.

"Sorry," she mumbled.

"No worries," I said, because I liked the way Tommy sounded when he said it. "Your turn, Storm."

"Okay. Well, remember that time we docked in

the cove, right next to that ninety-foot yacht? The HMS *Snobbysnot*?"

I nodded. "The rich kids whose parents couldn't figure out how to get their fancy diesel engines running."

"Right. Anyway, Dad was on the deck, cleaning up a dagger he'd found in that sunken pirate ship. It was such a hot day I jumped in for a swim. That's when the bratty boys on the yacht started in with the walrus and blubber jokes."

Tommy laughed. "I remember that! Dad clenched the dagger between his teeth, grabbed a rope, and went swinging over to the yacht, pirate-style."

Beck picked it up from there. "Then he said, 'You folks look like you're having engine problems. Too bad you're miles from the nearest mechanic. Just about the only person who might be able to help you out is my beautiful daughter, the pretty girl swimming down there.'"

Storm was biting back her tears.

So I went ahead and finished her story for her: "'Because,' Dad said, 'just for fun, Storm Kidd has memorized the maintenance and repair manuals for just about every seagoing craft there is. Including *your* floating mansion.'"

"And then you fixed their engines," said Tommy.

"Only because Dad asked me to," said Storm, trying to dry her eyes with her knuckles. "It's what we 'beautiful' daughters do. Okay, Tommy. Your turn."

Tommy fumbled with the hat in his hands. "Okay. Um, thanks, Dad, and, uh, thanks, Mom, for, you know...*everything*."

We all nodded. Because that pretty much summed it up.

Tommy tossed Dad's hat into the sea.

And we all stood on the deck, watching it slowly float away.

CHAPTER 3

There's something else you should know about Beck and me: We sometimes erupt into what our parents used to call Twin Tirades.

Of course, when Mom and Dad first called it that, I didn't even know what a tirade was.

So, Mom (our homeschool ELA teacher) made me look it up: "Tirade: a prolonged outburst of bitter, angry words."

Basically, there's lots of shouting and snippy name-calling (the names I come up with are way better than Beck's—I'm the writer; she's the artist).

And our Twin Tirades aren't really "prolonged." In fact, they usually last about sixty seconds and then we're done. They're sort of like a summer squall in the Bahamas. Lots of thunder and lightning and then, a minute later, the sky's completely clear.

Anyway, Rebecca (I call her that only when I'm mad) and I burst into a Twin Tirade while we were lugging bailing buckets up from the engine room.

"We need a plan, Bick," she said, coming to such an abrupt halt in the deckhouse that water sloshed out of both of her buckets.

"Tommy has a plan," I said. "We ride the current up to the Caymans. That's where the treasure is."

"I'm talking about the bigger picture, Bickford!" (Yep, she only calls me Bickford when she's angry, too.)

"I thought you said we needed a plan, not a picture, Rebecca!"

"That *is* what I said. And it has to be the

absolute best plan. Not the second-best. The *best*!"

"Well, who's going to decide what's absolutely best for us?"

"We are!"

"And by *we*," I said, "do you, by any chance, mean *you*, Miss Bossypants?"

"No, you numskull!" Beck's face was redder

than a boiled lobster. "If I meant *me*, I would have said *me*, not *we*."

"What about Tommy and Storm?"

"They're part of *we* and *us*."

"No, they're not. Do the math, Einstein. We're twins. Not quadruplets."

"I mean *us* us. The whole family."

"Then why didn't you say so?"

"I already did."

"When?"

"Just now."

"Really?"

"Yeah."

"Oh. Sorry."

"That's okay."

"Are we cool?"

"Totally."

And, just like that, our Twin Tirade was done.

Together, we made our way out of the cabin and into the wheelhouse.

"Tommy?" said Beck.

"Storm?" I called.

"We need a plan!" we shouted together.

Tommy nodded. "Cool. I'm down with that."

Storm emptied her bailing bucket over the side and joined us on the poop deck.

"What's the plan?" she asked.

"First, we survive!" I said.

"Okay," said Tommy. "How's that gonna happen?"

"Easy," said Beck. "Mom and Dad taught us everything we need to know."

Storm nodded, and soon Tommy was nodding, too.

"We'll need to start rationing the food and drinking water," Storm said. "I'll work up a spreadsheet on the computer."

"And I'll check out the stars tonight," said Tommy. "Triangulate a little. Make sure this current is taking us where we need to be."

The two of them turned to Beck and me. "Then what?" they said together.

It looked like our big brother and sister were

ready for Beck and me to take charge of this barely floating disaster.

"Well," I said, "we keep doing what we've always done."

Tommy arched an eyebrow. "Treasure hunting?"

"Without Mom and Dad?" said Storm.

"Why not?" said Beck.

"It's our family business," I said, completing her thought. (Yeah, that's something else twins do.) "We just need to find Dad's treasure map for the Cayman dive."

"And don't forget," said Beck, "we already know how to do everything that needs to be done. We can maintain the ship. We can fish and forage for food."

"And Tommy can navigate us anywhere on the seven seas," I said.

He nodded as humbly as he could. "True, true."

"And, Storm," said Beck, "you can handle all the computer stuff."

"And evaluate potential new treasure sites," Storm added.

"I can cut deals with suppliers over the Internet," said Beck, "once Tommy fixes our satellite dish."

"Top of my list," said Tommy, "soon as we reach port. Satellite dish and a cheeseburger. With fries."

"We don't really need any adults to keep this business afloat," I added. "Besides, does anybody here really want to give up treasure hunting? Do any of us seriously want to live a boring landlubber life filled with schools, strip malls, and frozen fish sticks?"

We all shook our heads.

Beck tossed in a gag-me-now gesture.

The truth was, none of us could ever be happy on dry land, not after having spent the bulk of our lives adventuring on the high seas. Heck, we'd even met pirates. Real ones. Not the wax kind at Disney World.

In a way, we Kidd kids were like the wild

things in this picture book my dad always read to Beck and me when we were little. The one where an ocean tumbled by with a private boat and a boy named Max sailed off through night and day.

"We can do this," said Beck.

"Definitely," said Tommy.

"No doubt," echoed Storm.

I stepped forward. "All those in favor of keeping Kidd Family Treasure Hunters Inc. open for business, raise your hand."

CHAPTER 4

The best thing about sunset at sea?

It's not the pretty colors. It's the fact that the freakishly hot fireball in the sky finally stops sizzling you like a strip of extracrispy bacon when it

dips down into the ocean. If you squint, you can see steam rising.

We made it to nightfall, which definitely helped with the heat. Except belowdecks. The cabins down there were like ovens with bunk beds. So, while Tommy manned the wheel up top and Storm went down to the galley to check out what kind of food supplies we had left in the pantry, Beck and I started to hatch our survival plan in the coolest place we could find. We made our way into the cluttered room at the windowed front of the deckhouse—what our boat builders back in Hong Kong called the "lavish grand salon" in their sales brochures.

With us, it was more like the messy rumpus room. True, the room had, as advertised, "a curved couch, sleek teak paneling, and hardwood cabinetry with a built-in sink." But the sink had dirty dishes and empty soda bottles in it, the paneled walls were cluttered with a collection of my parents' favorite treasures (including a conquistador helmet, a rare African tribal mask, a grog jug shaped like a frog, a rusty cannonball

from a Confederate gunboat, a bronze clock covered with cherubs that probably belonged to King Louis XIV, and, in a glass shadow box, a rusty steak knife from the *Titanic*).

There were assorted trinkets, necklaces, and coconut heads suspended from the ceiling. Add a heap of scuba and snorkel gear and assorted socks, shoes, and T-shirts on the floor (the floor is our laundry basket), and our grand salon looked more like a live-in recycling bin.

"Have we even seen a map for this treasure hunt?" asked Beck.

"Nope. Dad just said we needed to be in the Caymans."

"Then we need to find his map."

After about an hour of searching in the junk heap—made even junkier by the tropical storm that had knocked a bunch of stuff off the table, walls, and counters—I hit upon an idea. I turned to Beck with a determined look in my eye.

(I said "determined," Beck, not "demented." You know the look I'm talking about.)

(That's better.)

"We need to look in The Room," I whispered.

"We can't go into The Room," Beck whispered back. "The Room is locked."

"Then we need to find The Key to The Room."

Yes, every time any of us talk about The Room or The Key to The Room, it always comes out sounding like we're talking in capital letters, because The Room is off-limits to *All Of Us*. It also has a solid steel door with a serious dead bolt—the same kind of lock used on bank vaults. At Fort Knox.

The Room is where Mom and Dad kept the most secret stuff on the boat. Treasure maps.

Retrieval plans. Notes on dealers and middlemen for museums.

But getting our hands on all that wasn't my only reason for wanting to break one of our parents' most important rules by busting into The Room.

"Beck? If I tell you something, promise you won't think I'm crazy?"

"Sorry. Already do."

So I went ahead and told her anyway: "I think Dad might be in there. Alive."

CHAPTER 5

"You're kidding, right?"

This was not the reaction I'd been looking for.

"This isn't a joke, Beck," I said as we made our way belowdecks and headed toward the bow.

The Room was in the forward-most section of the hull. We stood in front of The Door staring at The Lock.

"Maybe Dad went in there during the storm, maybe to secure some extremely important documents or seal a treasure map inside a watertight container, when, all of a sudden, a wave slammed into the side of the boat, knocked something off a shelf, and—BAM!—he got conked on the head, and he's been knocked out ever since."

Beck just looked at me. "Seriously?"

"It's possible."

"Then why didn't we see him, Bick? Hello? We were standing right here in the hallway, remember? If not, allow me to refresh your memory." She made a bunch of *splash-splash-gurgle-gurgle* noises. "We were up to our necks in water, and I don't remember seeing Dad swim past us so he could sneak into The Room."

"You weren't there the whole time. Maybe he used one of the secret hatches up on deck."

Oh, in case I forgot to mention it, *The Lost* has been customized with all sorts of secret hatches, trapdoors, and hiding places. It helps when you're hauling treasure in pirate-infested waters to have someplace safe to stow your precious cargo. Beck can't show you exactly where all these compartments, hollowed-out masts, and secret passageways are, or—duh—they wouldn't be secret, but this will give you the gist.

Anyway, once I mentioned my Dad-sneaked-in-through-a-secret-trapdoor-in-the-deck idea, Beck got a look in her eyes, and I knew: It was time for Twin Tirade No. 426.

"Give it up, Bickford. Dad is dead!"

"No, he's not, Rebecca. He's in The Room."

"No. Way."

"It's possible."

"Yeah. Just like you facing reality someday. It's *possible*."

"I'll bet he's in there, right now, lying on the floor."

"He's dead, Bick."

"No, he'll just look that way."

"Because he *is*!"

"He's probably thirsty and hungry, too."

"No, he's not."

"Of course he is! We should make him a sandwich. Maybe bring him a sports drink."

"He's not hungry or thirsty, Bickford, because he's dead. It's one of the few advantages of dying: You don't have to eat or drink or do the dishes."

"Rebecca, how can you be so cold and heartless?"

"How can you be so sentimental?"

"Easy. I have a heart."

"Too bad it's not pumping blood to your brain, dum-dum."

"Sorry, Mrs. Spock. We can't all be superlogical like you."

"I'd settle for semilogical."

"Really?"

"Yeah."

"Oh. Okay."

"Cool."

Yep. Twenty seconds, and we were done.

"Sorry," I said.

"Ditto," said Beck.

"Is anybody going to apologize to me?" Storm trudged into the hallway from the cabin she shares with Beck. "I was trying to sleep."

"I thought you were making a list of our food supplies," said Beck.

"It took about two seconds because we have

55

about *nada*. I decided to take a nap instead. And now thanks to you two, I'm awake. What're you two doing?"

"We need to get into The Room," I said.

"Why?"

"To find Dad's treasure map for the Caymans dive."

THE ROOM.

SOLID STEEL

← THE LOCK

Storm made a fish-lips face and thought about that for a couple of seconds. "Good idea." Then, yawning and scratching her butt, she turned around and shuffled back into her cabin.

"Okay," I said to Beck, "if you were Dad, where would you hide The Key?"

Before Beck could answer, Storm trudged back into the hall holding a windup alarm clock. She slammed it against that hardwood paneling I told you about earlier. Glass shattered. Tiny pieces went flying everywhere.

And a brass key tumbled to the floor.

CHAPTER 6

First off, I was totally wrong.

Dad was *not* lying unconscious and starving on the floor of The Room. (So, room service, cancel the sandwich and refreshing beverage.)

The cabin was windowless and dark. So dark, Beck (temporarily) took off her 3-D glasses. But even though we saw nothing but murky shadows, we both knew that The Room was where Mom and Dad kept the treasures of our treasure-hunting enterprise.

I found a wall sconce and switched it on.

"Wow," Beck and I said simultaneously.

"This is incredible," I said. In the dim light, I could see that the walls were covered with

corkboards. And the corkboards were cluttered with all sorts of pinned-up papers and photographs and maps.

"There's the three-hundred-year-old icon we returned to that Orthodox church on Cyprus right before Mom disappeared," said Beck, pointing to a photograph. "And the thank-you note from the bishop of Neapolis."

"These are all the medieval sword hilts and scabbards we salvaged off the coast of England," I said, working my way through the photographs pegged to the wall on the other side of The Room.

The cabinets beneath the jumbled bulletin boards had chicken-wire-mesh fronts instead of glass and held all sorts of priceless art, artifacts, and antiquities. Pre-Columbian pottery. Ancient weapons. Chubby Buddhas carved out of jade. A shattered clay jar filled with Venetian silver coins. A brass incense burner shaped like a Hindu goddess.

There was even a golden, bull-headed mummy's sarcophagus secured in the corner of The Room, right behind The Door.

Beck was staring at a map on the wall behind the cabinets.

"There's not an inch to spare in here," said Beck. "So why is this thing taking up half a wall?"

It was a simple, schoolroom-style pull-down map of North and Central America. There were no chart markings on it. The Cayman Islands were barely visible south of Cuba.

"And check this out," I said, pointing to a handwritten list tucked under the glass blotter on top of Mom and Dad's desk:

TO-DO LiST:

1. Secret city of Paititi (The Real City of Gold)
2. King Solomon's Mines
3. The Cave of the House of Hakkoz
4. The Crown Jewels of King John
5. The "Flower of the Sea" Portuguese Frigate
6. The Lost Fabergé Eggs of Saint Petersburg
7. San Miguel & the 1715 Treasure Fleet
8. The Amber Room of the Catherine Palace
9. The treasure of the Knights Templar
10. Marie Antoinette's Missing jewelry

"Big whoop," said Beck. "That's a top ten list of the world's greatest missing treasures. Weren't you paying attention when Mom taught us about this stuff in geography class?"

"Uh, yeah. But this isn't just a list, Beck. It's a *to-do* list. This is what Mom and Dad were planning for the future."

Beck shrugged. "I guess they were trying to figure out how to pay for *four* college educations."

"Not that any of us would ever be interested in college," I reminded her.

"Speak for yourself," she said. Totally unimpressed with the mind-blowing list I had just uncovered, Beck went back to checking out the wall behind the desk. The half not taken up by the map was filled with photographs and printouts of art—paintings, statues, and pottery. Beck was focused on the paintings.

"That's a Renoir," she said, pointing at one of the paintings. She knows this stuff because whenever we're in a major port city, she spends all her time in the museums—she's the family "artiste," after all. "A Manet. A Monet."

"How do you tell those two apart again?"

"Tiny paint dabs, it's Monet. Chubby Parisians, Manet."

"Right."

"That one there is a Degas. Next to it is a Cézanne. And a Gauguin. A Picasso. And a Van Gogh—one that's been missing for years."

"You think Mom and Dad were planning on going after all these?"

"If they were, they'd have had to steal them. Huh. Maybe that's why this is up here." Beck tapped on a black-and-white photograph of a smiling gangster wearing an old-fashioned fedora hat and chomping on a cigar. "To remind us *not* to hunt down any of these treasures."

Next to the mug shot of the mobster was a copy of the *Chicago Sunday Tribune* from October 18, 1931. The banner headline shouted JURY CONVICTS CAPONE.

While Beck studied the art masterpieces, I checked out a different kind of art—a cartoon that Dad had tucked under the glass near the to-do list. I knew it was Dad who clipped the comic out of some magazine because it was based on this very lame joke he must've told me a million times: A professor, in his cap and gown, is showing a head-scratching student an ancient Greek vase with figures and scenes painted all over its sides. "What's a Grecian urn?" asks the student. The professor's answer? "About thirty dollars a week."

Corniest. Joke. In. The. World.

But for the past couple of months, my dad had *loved* telling it. To me. Over and over and over again. It was like the Greek version of Chinese water torture.

He'd even scribbled a note in the margins of the cartoon: "That is all ye need to know, matey." He must've written it during National Write Like a Pirate Week.

Beck and I searched The Room for fifteen or twenty more minutes, but neither one of us could find anything resembling a map for a Cayman

Islands treasure hunt. And there was nothing pinned to the bulletin boards about shipwrecks off the coast of the Caymans or secret lost Cayman cities of gold or even a take-out menu for Cayman jerk chicken.

"So, Bick?"

"Yeah, Beck?"

"All this stuff is extremely cool."

"Extremely."

"I only have one question."

I nodded. "Same here."

"How come Storm knew where Dad had hidden The Key?"

We said *that* at the same time, too.

CHAPTER 7

Beck and I stormed (sorry about that) into Storm's cabin.

She was sitting on the lower bunk, flipping through the pages of a six-inch-thick hardbound book the way a fast-scanning copy machine would.

"International maritime law," she mumbled as she finished the whole book in, like, fifteen seconds. "Fascinating stuff."

"Storm?" said Beck.

Storm looked up at Beck with sleepy eyes and said nothing.

"How come you knew where The Key was hidden?" I demanded.

"Because I have a photographic memory."

"What's *that* got to do with *this*?" I jiggle-dangled The Key in front of my face.

Storm shrugged. "Dad didn't trust himself to remember where he hid it. So he asked me to be his designated key keeper."

"Wha-what?" Beck sputtered a little when she heard that. "You and Dad? Together? Hid it?"

(You see why it's a good thing Beck is such an excellent artist? Her verbal skills are...a little weak. What? No, I will not write that my personal-hygiene skills are also a little weak. Oh. I just did. Shoot.)

"What else were you and Dad hiding from us?" asked Beck.

"Um, let's see." She held up her very thick law book. "He asked me to 'familiarize' myself with this book's contents. Said it might come in handy when we hit the Caymans."

"Have you ever been inside The Room?" I asked.

"Nope. I was just in charge of hiding The Key and not forgetting where I hid it. So give it back, Bick. I need to hide it again."

"No, you don't," said Beck. "We need The Room."

68

"For what?"

"Files and stuff."

"Did you find a treasure map for a Caymans dive?"

"No," muttered Beck.

"Not yet, anyway," I added.

"Maybe Tommy knows where Dad put it," said Storm. "He's been in The Room a couple of times."

Now it was my turn to stammer. "Wh-whaaa?"

"Him and Dad. Once, they wanted to go in after I had hidden The Key in the bottom of the cookie jar. Squirreled it underneath all the Oreos and Mallomars. Best hiding place *ever*."

"So you knew about The Key," I said, "and Tommy's been in The Room. What else don't we know?"

"Well," said Storm, "Mom told me you both needed to work harder on your trig homework and—"

Suddenly, an air horn blared up on deck.

WHOMP! WHOMP! WHOMP!

Kidd Family Rule No. 1: If you hear the air horn do a triple blast, drop everything, no matter what you're doing, and race to the deck. A triple blast means somebody's in trouble and needs help. (Two toots means "Dinner's ready," and four, "The Dolphins won the Super Bowl.")

The three of us hurried up out of the hull quarters, dashed across the deckhouse, and scrambled up the ladder to the wheelhouse.

Tommy nodded toward our stern and raised a pair of binoculars up to his eyes.

SOMETHING WICKED THIS WAY SAILS!

"We have company," said Tommy.

Every time the waves behind us rolled down, I could see a boat racing across the heaving white-caps. When the waves swelled, it disappeared. When they dropped again, it had moved closer.

"Uh, Tommy?" I said.

"Yeah?"

"This may not be the best time to ask...."

"Go ahead, little bro," said Tommy, never taking his eyes off the boat, which definitely seemed to be gaining on us. "We've got time. Couple of minutes, anyway."

The white-hot searchlight swung across our stern, then swooped back and tilted up. Beck, Storm, and I looked like deer caught in the head-lights of an oncoming freight train. Tommy did not. He narrowed his eyes down to slits.

"Um, okay. So, why did Dad take you into The Room?"

"No big deal," said Tommy, keeping his eyes glued to the speedboat (we could hear its whining engines now) bounding over the foamy breakers behind us. "He just needed to tell me some oldest-kid stuff."

"Really? Like what?"

"Like where he kept the spare speargun."

Without taking his eyes off the snarling speedboat, which was only about twenty yards behind us now, Tommy tapped the baseboard of the wheelhouse wall with his right foot. A narrow cabinet popped open.

Inside was what looked like a rocket launcher equipped with a lethal, twin-barbed shaft.

You know—oldest-kid stuff.

CHAPTER 8

"Wha happen, my friends?" shouted the man behind the wheel of the speedboat as he pulled back on the throttles and eased his craft alongside our starboard. He held up both his hands. "And, please, do not point that speargun at me, Bobo. I am not a fish." And then he let loose with a rumbling Caribbean laugh. "Ah-ha-ha-ha-ha."

The man in the speedboat was wearing a weird collection of clothes: A policeman's cap with a bright red band above its shiny black brim, a sleeveless tuxedo jacket (but no tuxedo shirt), a necklace made out of shark teeth, and brightly striped pajama pants.

And did I mention the blue iguana nibbling lettuce leaves in a cage on the passenger seat of his banana-yellow speedboat?

"Please, brudda," he said, gesturing at the iguana, "lower the speargun. You are scaring Tedee."

"Who are you?" demanded Tommy.

"Why, I am the man who just found *you* lost on *The Lost* in the middle of the sea. Ah-ha-ha-ha."

Storm moved behind Tommy. Guess she didn't like the jolly man's laugh.

Or maybe it was the tattoos running up and down both of his bulging arms. Could've been the scar slashing his left cheek, too. Or the fact that he'd ripped the sleeves off a perfectly good tuxedo jacket.

"Help me out, little brudda," the guy called to me, I guess because I was at the railing closest to him. He held a mooring line in his hands and gestured like he wanted to toss it to me.

I looked to Tommy.

He shook his head.

I stayed where I was.

"My friends," he said, dropping the coiled rope, "I mean you no harm. If I did, I would have shown you this instead of a rope."

He raised a nasty-looking rifle with a curved ammunition clip.

"That's an AK-47," whispered Storm. "Originally developed in the USSR by Mikhail Kalashnikov, it fires a thirty-nine-millimeter cartridge with a muzzle velocity of seven hundred and fifteen

meters per second. *Modern Ammo Magazine*, June 1987. It totally beats a speargun, Tommy."

Tommy lowered his weapon. Our visitor lowered his.

"Your boat," he said, "she is not looking so good, eh?"

"We had a little trouble in the storm," said Tommy.

"Ah. This would explain your delay. Where is Thomas Kidd?"

"I'm Tommy Kidd."

"Dr. Thomas Kidd? The world-famous treasure hunter? This is you?"

"That's our dad!" I shouted. "He's not here right now."

"Really? Oh, my. The Big Man will not be happy."

"Who is the Big Man?" said Beck, jutting out her hip and planting a hand on it just to give our visitor a little 'tude.

"The Big Man is the one who sent me all the way out here to find you, little lady."

"And how, exactly, did you do that?" I asked.

"Your transponder, little brudda. Your satellite and radio may not work, but your AIS radar beacon is looo-king good."

"Do we have that?" I asked out of the corner of my mouth.

"Yeah," said Tommy out of the corner of his. Guess that was more oldest-kid stuff.

"You see, Kidds, your father gave the Big Man your transponder numbers. When your father does not show up to deliver the goods, well, the Big Man, he sends me out to *find* the goods. Instead, I find *you*."

"Well," said Beck, "we don't know what kind of goods you're talking about."

"That's okay. The Big Man, he will know. You come with me, Tommy Kidd. You explain to the Big Man why he did not receive that which your father promised to deliver."

"No," I said. "We're family. We stick together."

"If Tommy goes," added Beck, "we all go."

"Heh-heh-heh. Very good. We *all* go see the Big Man."

He raised his coiled line again. This time Tommy nodded to say it was okay.

I scampered down the ladder.

"Tie me off to your bow, little brudda."

I grunted when I caught the heavy hemp line he heaved at my chest. Hauling the rope up to the foredeck, I looped it around a cleat and tied it off with a hitch knot. I raced down the deck and joined everybody else up in

the wheelhouse. The instant I got there, I heard engines rev.

The speedboat shot forward and fishtailed in front of us.

"What's going on, Tommy?" I asked as *The Lost* cut across the souped-up tugboat's choppy wake.

"Dude in the tuxedo is giving us a free ride up to Grand Cayman, which is where we want to be. This way, we save on gas."

"Oh. Okay. Cool."

But something told me that being "found" might turn out to be more dangerous than staying "lost."

CHAPTER 9

The next morning, when we woke up in Grand Cayman, I expected us to be docked next to boatloads of scurvy knaves, all of them toting AK-47s, machetes, or worse.

Instead, we were moored in a very swanky marina, our battered boat surrounded by gleaming yachts and sleek sailboats.

"Good morning, Kidds," boomed our jolly tugboat captain as he climbed aboard *The Lost* at first light with a green parrot perched on his shoulder. I guessed the iguana had the day off. "I brought ackee and salt fish for everybody!"

"What?" asked Storm.

"It is a very popular traditional breakfast here in the Caymans."

"Was the store all out of Froot Loops?"

"Come on, Storm," said Beck. "Try it."

(For the record, breakfast did not look that good to anybody except Beck. Seriously, who eats fish for breakfast besides bigger fish?)

After choking the food down (and wishing I had some Tic Tacs), we were driven into George Town for our audience with the Big Man, which, apparently, was going to take place at a dump with a tin roof called the Surf Shack.

"Wait a second," said Tommy as we all piled out of Jolly Mon's dusty Range Rover. "We've been here before. Back when the twins were *way* younger."

"It was six years ago," said Storm. "The second Tuesday in July. Temperature was eighty-three degrees, and there was a sudden downpour at three fifteen in the afternoon. Tommy got a surfboard. Beck and Bick got boogie boards. I tried jerk chicken egg rolls for the first time, and they were amazing."

The Surf Shack was part surf shop, part boat shop, part disgusting restaurant, and, I'm pretty sure, part black-market front. I vaguely recall Mom and Dad bartering for our boogie boards with booty they'd brought up from a shipwreck off the coast of Jamaica.

The parrot squawked on Jolly Mon's shoulder.

"Ah, here he is! The Big Man himself."

A burly, three-hundred-pound guy in dark sunglasses—with a bald dome ringed by wet, curly hair—waddled out from the shadows. He was all smiles as he toddled off the Surf Shack's porch like a bear-sized penguin. Wearing a rumpled Hawaiian shirt (with dark half-moon sweat stains under each armpit), baggy cargo shorts, and heel-thwacking flip-flops, the guy looked vaguely familiar.

"Louie Louie?" said Tommy, his tensed shoulders sagging with relief.

"Oh, yes. In the flesh, as they say. In the flesh." Louie Louie slapped his jiggling jelly belly and

TODAY'S SPECIALS
- FOOD POISONING
- GREASY SPOONS
- FISH THAT WAS FRESH LAST WEEK
- SURLY WAITERS
- COFFEE THAT TASTES WORSE THAN MUD
THE SURF SHACK
SALE!
BLEH!

laughed. He sort of reminded me of Santa Claus. If Santa lived in a cheap beach motel, had body-odor issues, and listened to steel drums in a thatched tiki hut all day.

"My, my, my. So good to see you all again. It's been too long since we last had the entire Kidd clan here with us on Grand Cayman."

"Six years," said Storm drily. "And, just in case you hadn't noticed, Mom and Dad aren't here."

EW!

LOUIE LOUIE THE HUMAN SPRINKLER

"Ah, yes. Indeed. I had noticed that. Pity. Called off to another lecture, were they?"

"Something like that," said Beck. "Mr. Louie? Maybe we should talk about all this...inside?"

"Oh, yes. Inside. Capital suggestion. Get out of the sun. Enjoy some refreshing beverages. Order up a batch of deep-fried conch fritters, eh? Come, children. We have much to talk about. Very much, indeed. Thank you, Maurice."

He bowed slightly to the man who had towed us into harbor last night.

"Will you be needing anything else, Mr. L?"

"No. Not just now. Later, perhaps?"

"Ah, yes. Ah-ha-ha-ha." Maurice gave Louie Louie a two-finger salute off the tip of his castaway-cop cap and headed back to his Range Rover. We followed Louie Louie into his shady establishment.

"Shame your father was called off the boat so unexpectedly," said Mr. Louie as we followed him through the cluttered aisles of the Surf Shack. "He was bringing me something very special.

Very special, indeed. In fact, we had a very firm deal, as I recall."

"Hey," said Tommy, trying to change the subject, "I see you still have that autographed Duke Kahanamoku surfboard."

"Oh, yes. Been there for years."

"I used to think it was called the Don't-Touch-That surfboard," Tommy joked.

"Children. Such a delight," said Mr. Louie, rumbling up a chuckle. He took off his sunglasses (which had an oil slick where they'd been bumping into his eyebrows) and darted his beady eyes back and forth slyly. "Would you like to touch the surfboard today, Tommy?"

"Really?"

"Absolutely. I think it will prove most beneficial to our upcoming business discussion."

Tommy shrugged. "Sure. Whatever."

He stroked the tail fins.

I heard a click.

Suddenly, the whole wall behind the famous surfboard started to slide open, revealing a set of hidden steps that led down into a dark cellar.

"Step into my office, Kidds," said Louie Louie, gesturing toward the staircase and wiping sweat off his shiny head. "We have some serious business matters to discuss. Very serious, indeed."

Now we were sweating, too.

GREAT. A DARK BASEMENT.
NOTHING SCARY OR CREEPY ABOUT THAT.

CHAPTER 10

L ouie Louie's secret downstairs lair was chock-full of treasures and antiquities.

I saw golden chalices, a jewel-studded crown, a couple of Grecian urns (Dad would've told me his corny joke again), a full suit of armor, Byzantine brooches, pirate swords, a crate filled with pearls, a collection of colorful glass bottles, and water-stained sea chests brimming with jewelry and gold doubloons (just like you'd see bubbling in the bottom of an aquarium).

"Where'd you get all this stuff?" I asked.

"From those who, shall we say, wished to exchange it for something *greener*." Louie Louie chortled and jiggled. "Cold, hard cash."

"So you're basically a fence?" said Storm, who, like I've said before, isn't big on thinking before speaking. "A person who deals with stolen goods?"

"Oh, no. I am but a humble businessman. I am one who will do business with anyone who cares to do business with me. For instance, your father."

Even though it was just him and us in the cluttered basement, Louie Louie made a big show of looking around to make certain no one else was listening to what he said next.

"I have a certain...*item*...that your father was most desirous of possessing. An insignificant trinket, actually. A mere Minoan bauble at best. It is an amulet. Half the face of some insect god or goddess. Worthless, actually, without its matching twin. Be that as it may, your father informed me, in the strictest confidence, that this *item* was of vital importance. Something to do with a terrible mess he and your mother were tangled up in? Tell me, children, has your mother really gone missing somewhere in Cyprus?"

The four of us shot glances back and forth.

GOLDEN FLEECE

GOLDEN FLEAS

THE MISSING POCAHONTAS SOUVENIR GLASS FROM THAT BURGER KING PROMOTION

SOMEBODY'S STOLEN BASEBALL CARDS

How much does Louie Louie know about Dad's business and Mom's disappearance?

I was about to evade the question with some kind of clever response, but Storm blurted out her answer first.

"They're both dead. Mom in Cyprus. Dad in the storm."

Louie Louie acted stunned and surprised.

But I think I saw the twitch of a grin.

"Really?" he said, clutching both of his chubby hands over his heart. "Oh, dear. Oh, my. The four of you are...*orphans*?"

"Yeah," said Beck, putting on her tough act. "But we're still in business."

"Indeed? Tell me: Do the authorities here in port know that you are currently without adult supervision or guardianship?"

"No," I said.

"Oh, my. I suppose the local orphanage might take you in."

Tommy stepped forward. "Are you trying to scare us, sir?"

"Me? Scare poor, defenseless orphans? Heavens,

no. However, as a friend of the family, I feel I must warn you—you're not safe in the Caymans."

"Why not?"

"Well, first off, there's the orphan situation we were just discussing. And I have heard rumors of pirates who seem quite interested in your father and certain items on board *The Lost.*"

"Do these pirates want what Dad was bringing you?" asked Beck.

"Perhaps. It is quite valuable."

"Then *you* should be afraid of them, too."

"You raise a good point. However, there is something else."

"More danger?" I asked, because it seemed to be lurking around every corner.

"Oh, yes. A very dangerous man has just arrived in George Town. A man you may wish to avoid. He's coming here to see me in, oh, about an hour."

"Who is it?" demanded Tommy.

Louie Louie's grin twitched up a notch into a full-fledged smirk. "Nathan Collier."

When we heard that name, the four of us gasped.

CHAPTER 11

Nathan Collier was our dad's number one nemesis. His archrival. Collier, another treasure hunter, was forever trying to snatch our finds out from under us or take credit for discoveries we'd already made, because he wasn't very good at bringing anything up from a dive besides old tires.

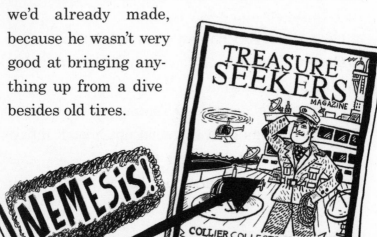

#1 NEMESIS!

TREASURE SEEKERS MAGAZINE

COLLIER COLLECTS CURIOUS COMMEMORATIVE COINS!

"You're doing business with Collier?" said Beck.

"As I said, I am a businessman eager to do business with those eager to do business with me."

"I thought you were our parents' friend."

"Oh, I was. Unfortunately, as Storm so eloquently pointed out, your parents are no longer, shall we say, *available* for me to be friends with. Perhaps Nathan Collier can find the item I so desperately desire. As I mentioned, he will be arriving in under an hour to discuss the matter."

"You don't need Collier," I said. "If Dad said he was bringing you your treasure, then it's definitely on *The Lost*."

"Bick's right," said Beck. "We'll honor your agreement with Dad. But you don't get to take home your treasure till you hire a crew to fix up our boat."

Even though she's only twelve years old, Beck is, if you ask me, one of the toughest negotiators in the world. My twin sister could talk a dog off a meat truck.

"Such demands. Oh, my." Louie was chuckling

so much his blubbery cheeks were shimmying. "Very amusing. Very amusing, indeed. But tell me, little girl: Why should *I* pay workers to fix *your* boat?"

"First, Mr. Louie, my name is Rebecca. Second, because *The Lost* needs repairs and you need whatever it was that Dad was bringing you."

"But I am offering you the amulet he desired."

"Yes, sir, but you messed up. First, you called this amulet a 'trinket' and a 'bauble.' You even said it was 'worthless.' On the other hand, the item Dad was bringing you is a 'treasure.' Now that you've shown us your hand, the only way to make this a fair swap is for you to, you know..."

I gave Beck the words she was looking for: "You need to sweeten the pot."

"Exactly," said Beck. "Sweeten the pot with a couple of days of free boat repairs. You find a fix-up crew to work on *The Lost* for two days. When they're done, we give you your 'treasure.'"

"My, my, my. You drive a hard bargain."

Beck shrugged. "I am my mother's daughter. Deal or no deal?"

Louie Louie ran his tongue across his upper lip to swipe away some of the sweat beading there. "Deal. But, Rebecca, if I do not find what I am looking for on board your ship, if I am disappointed in *any* way, you four will owe me the full cost of the repairs. Do you have sufficient cash to cover such an enormous expense?"

"Of course we do," Beck bluffed. "We had an excellent year."

"Good. Because if you fail to satisfy the terms of our agreement, I will, with the assistance of my good friend Maurice, simply take possession of *The Lost*."

In other words, two days from now, if we didn't give Louie Louie what he wanted and couldn't pay for the repairs, he and his iguana-loving buddy with the AK-47 would come take our boat away from us.

Bye-bye, Kidd Family Treasure Hunters Inc.

Beck looked around the room.

We all nodded in agreement. We didn't have much of a choice.

"Deal," she said.

She reached out for Louie Louie's clammy paw.

They shook on it.

Poor Beck.

There wasn't enough Purell in the world to wash away the germs a slimy guy like Louie Louie left behind.

CHAPTER 12

For the next couple of days, Louie Louie's crew crawled all over *The Lost*, fixing up holes in the hull, patching up sails, rewiring fried electrical circuits. Fortunately, neither Nathan Collier nor the local orphanage officials came snooping around our dock.

I had a feeling that Jolly Mon and his blue iguana copilot had towed us to this particular marina because they knew it would be a good place to hole up. Nobody asked a lot of questions about us or our beat-up motor sailer.

But there was one girl, maybe nineteen years old, who *did* pay a lot of attention to everything happening on *The Lost*. Her sporty little pleasure yacht just happened to be docked in the marina slip right next to ours.

Actually, she only paid attention when Tailspin Tommy was up on deck.

The girl, whose name was Daphne, spent most of her time sunbathing.

"Y'all workin' on your boat?" she drawled in a soft Southern accent the first morning fifteen guys showed up with toolboxes, hammers, and saws to—DUH!—*work on our boat.*

"Yeah," said Tommy, grabbing hold of a jib line so his chest and arm muscles would flex more impressively. "We ran into some gnarly weather."

"That storm the other night?"

"Yeah," said Tommy. "It was tough. But *The Lost*? She can handle just about anything. I like a girl like that."

That's when Daphne sat up and started fanning her face with her copy of *Modern Tanning* magazine.

Beck and I were working up on the poop deck. I had a brush and a bucket of paint. I was glad I had the bucket. I thought I might hurl.

"I would just *love* to take a look around inside y'all's ship sometime," said Daphne.

"How about now?"

"Why, that'd be just awesome, Tommy!" Daphne slung her beach bag over her shoulder and sort of wiggle-skipped toward the stern of her boat while Tommy made manly strides toward ours.

I turned to Beck, and I could tell we were both thinking the same thing: *Intruder Alert.*

We dropped our tools, scrambled down the ladder, and followed Tommy and Daphne into the deckhouse.

"We picked that puppy up off the coast of Peru."

"Oh, my," gushed Daphne.

"Okay," said Beck, clapping her hands. "Tour's over. Our floating museum is officially closed."

"Beck?" said Tommy. "Knock it off."

Beck kept going. "You need to leave, lady."

"I beg your pardon?" Daphne fluttered her eye-lashes.

"Scram," I said. "Beat it."

Tommy pretended to chuckle. "Kids. Aren't they adorable? They don't mean what they're saying."

"Actually," I said, "we do."

"What's going on up here?" said Storm, climbing up from the hull.

"These two...children...are being extremely
rude!" While Daphne did her whole *why-I-never!* bit,
Storm scanned the walls the way she had scanned
that law book. She whipped around and shot a look
at Beck, who was standing closest to what Dad
used to call our "Pirate Protection" closet.

Beck popped it open.

And pulled out Dad's double-barreled shotgun.

Which she aimed right at Daphne's heart.

Those polka dots on her bikini top made an excellent target.

CHAPTER 13

"You wouldn't!" Tommy said to Beck.

"Oh yes, I would."

"Tommy!" shrieked Daphne. "Do something!"

I do declare.
I believe I am
fixin' to have the
vapors, Tommy!

"What's missing, Storm?" I asked while Beck kept the shotgun trained on Daphne.

"The *mwana pwo* African mask."

"Check her beach bag," barked Beck.

I was about to do it when Tommy snatched the canvas sack off Daphne's shoulder.

The African mask was in the bag.

"Daphne?" Tommy sounded heartbroken as he gingerly picked up the mask and handed it to Storm. "Were you trying to steal this?"

"Of course not, silly. I just thought it might be fun for Halloween."

"Seriously?" I said. "You expect us to buy that?"

"You can 'buy' whatever you like, you saucy little brat."

And with that, Daphne snatched her bag, turned on her heel, and sashayed out the door.

About ten minutes later, we heard her fire up her engines and putter out of the marina.

"Sorry about that, you guys," said Tommy as we all stood on the deck and watched Daphne's yacht disappear. "What an airhead."

"Um, are you talking about Daphne or you?" cracked Beck.

"Both," said Tommy, draping his arms over our shoulders. "I'm just a wonderful dunder-head."

That made all of us smile because that's what Mom and Dad used to call Tailspin Tommy: their wonderful dunderhead. It's kind of like being a dunce. Only sweeter.

* * *

That night, over dinner, when all the repairs were finished, Storm dropped another one of her blunt bombshells:

"It's a good thing Louie Louie paid for all the repairs. We're broke."

"What?" said Beck.

"I've been crunching the numbers. We have enough money in the checkbook for four tanks of gas and a week's worth of groceries."

"Well," I said, "someone will give us a loan."

"Nope," said Storm. "We have absolutely no credit, anywhere."

"But Louie Louie's coming tomorrow. If we don't have the treasure Dad promised him, we'll have to pay for all these repairs."

"Which will be kind of hard to do without any money," said Tommy.

"Then what happens?" I asked.

"Easy," said Beck. "Louie Louie takes over *The Lost*."

What a joke, I thought. After all our trusty ship had been through, it might finally sink.

Right here at the dock.

CHAPTER 14

F irst thing the next morning, Louie Louie climbed aboard our boat.

"Good morning, Kidds!" He was wearing half a plate of salt fish and ackee down the front of his Hawaiian shirt. "My, my," he said, admiring *The Lost.* "The old girl cleans up nicely, eh?"

"The guys you hired did a good job," said Tommy, wiping his hands on an oily rag. He'd been down in the engine room, making certain we'd be ready to shove off the instant Mr. Louie was satisfied with his treasure.

"Oh, yes. Very skilled laborers. Very costly, too. Now, then, where is my treasure?"

"Well, sir," I said, "since we don't really know

what Dad was bringing you, we're also not sure where he stored it."

"Quite the conundrum, eh? Well, good thing I have a solution. Allow me a look around. You can trust Louie Louie."

I glanced over to Beck. She nodded tentatively, and so I led Louie into the deckhouse.

"Ah! Eureka! There it is."

Okay. Some days you just get lucky.

Louie Louie waddled into the grand parlor area and reached for...you guessed it...the *mwana pwo* African mask.

"Such a marvelous mask, don't you think? A true treasure!"

Apparently, Daphne the bathing beauty hadn't been such a dumb blond after all. "Well, then," said Louie Louie, "since I am a man of my word, here is the item your father so desperately desired." He reached into one of the pouch pockets on his baggy cargo shorts and pulled out a bronze pendant hanging off a golden chain.

"As you can undoubtedly tell, this poor little fellow is missing its mate. There should be a second figure on the left. Why your father so urgently desired half of a bronze bumblebee bau-

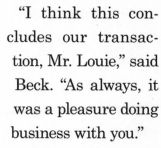

ble, we may never know."

"I think this concludes our transaction, Mr. Louie," said Beck. "As always, it was a pleasure doing business with you."

"Yes. Indeed." His little pig eyes darted around the parlor. "So much treasure. Might I examine that helmet more closely?"

"Sorry, sir," said Tommy. "We're hoisting anchor with the next high tide."

"Leaving so soon?"

"Yeah," said Beck. "We need to be somewhere else."

"May I inquire as to your destination?"

"Anywhere but here," I said.

"I see. Well, should you decide to seek, shall we say, loving homes for any more of this merchandise—"

"We'll give you a call," said Beck.

"Excellent. Farewell, Kidds. Again, my condolences on the loss of *both* of your parents." Louie turned around and leaped back to the dock, the mask already tucked into one of his many pockets.

As soon as Louie Louie was out of sight, Storm popped in her jeweler's eyepiece and examined the bronze bee pendant.

"This is very reminiscent of a Minoan bee pendant found outside the palace of Malia on the island of Crete. I can see locking slots for a second

set of feet above and below the circular beehive in the center."

"So, Louie was right," said Beck. "Somebody else has the other half."

Storm didn't answer.

Instead, she said, "Hello!"

"What've you got?" asked Tommy.

"Tiny latches. I need something to pry them open with."

I handed her my Swiss Army knife with the pointy file sticking out.

She flicked at the locket.

The bee's bloated belly popped open.

"Interesting," said Storm, switching to the knife's tweezers to pull something the size of a postage stamp out of the hollow cubbyhole.

"What is it?" I asked.

Storm held the tiny scrap of paper under her magnifying lens and smiled.

"A treasure map."

CHAPTER 15

We sailed out of port on the early-evening high tide.

While Tommy manned the wheel, I huddled with Storm and Beck in the deckhouse. We were transcribing the information from the miniature treasure map we'd found in the bee's belly onto an actual sea chart.

"No wonder Dad wanted this 'bronze bumblebee bauble,'" said Beck, doing her best Louie Louie impersonation. (It involved a lot of slobbery vowels.) "*This* is our Cayman Islands treasure map!"

"Do you guys know what this means?" I said.

"Uh, yeah," said Beck. "If we find this treasure,

we might be able to afford more than four tanks of gas and a couple sacks of groceries."

"Our troubles are over!" I raised both fists triumphantly. "Kidd Family Treasure Hunters Inc. is back in business."

"You might be right," said Storm, using her parallel rule and compass (the kind you probably use in geometry) to chart our course to the spot where the tiny map indicated that our treasure awaited. "There's a legend at the top of the miniature map."

"What's it say?" I asked eagerly.

"Córdoba's Lost Fleet."

Beck and I just leaned back in our chairs so Storm could school us from her five-billion-gigabyte memory of nautical history.

"In 1605, Córdoba's nine-vessel fleet sailed from Colombia bound for Havana. After just five days, they met up with a hurricane. Four galleons became separated from the rest of the fleet. Each of those four ships weighed more than five hundred tons, carried bronze cannons, and was loaded down with gold and silver bars from the New World. None of them has ever been found."

"Until now," said Beck.

As soon as Storm finished plotting our course, I rolled up the chart and raced it up to Tommy in the wheelhouse.

"It takes us straight to one of the galleons from the lost Córdoba fleet!"

"Sweet," said Tommy, because he always stays cooler than a cucumber sipping a Slurpee.

"Definitely."

Tommy nudged the wheel hard to the right. "We should be at the dive site by noon tomorrow."

"Awesome!" Everything was looking up.

Until I made the mistake of looking behind our boat to check out our wake.

Another speedboat was chasing after us. This one had all sorts of antennas and radar dishes on top of its pilothouse.

It also had a swirling red light.

"Uh, Tommy, I think we'd better pull over. It's the police."

CHAPTER 16

"What's going on, you guys?" said Beck, sticking her head out the deckhouse door. "Why are we slowing down?"

"Police," I said. "Don't worry. Tommy and I can handle this."

"Right," said Beck. "Like that's gonna happen." She slunk back down the steps. "Storm?" I heard her say. "I need your help on the computer."

"Cut your engines and drop anchor," said a very official voice with a British accent over the police boat's public-address speakers.

Tommy pulled back on the throttles and killed the engines. I raced up to the bow and lowered our anchor. When I returned to the stern of the ship, Tommy was chatting with a barrel-chested officer of the RCIPS—the Royal Cayman Islands Police Service.

The police officer was wearing a much cleaner version of the black hat with the red band that Maurice had worn the last time our boat was chased across the Caribbean. His crisp white shirt had shoulder boards and button-down pockets, one stuffed with what looked like parking tickets.

"Right," the officer said. "I'm Police Constable Jackson Wilmot. You are?"

"Tommy."

"Do you have a last name?"

"Definitely."

The cop lowered his sunglasses and arched his eyebrows to let Tommy know he'd like to hear what that last name was.

"Oh, right. Duh. Kidd. I'm Tommy Kidd. We were just, you know, out here, chillin'."

"Is that so?" said Constable Wilmot.

"We were going deep-sea fishing," I said with a great big, innocent smile.

Constable Wilmot flipped open a black leather ledger. "You would be Bickford Kidd, is that correct?"

"Yes, sir. How did you know my name?"

"An interested third party provided it to our Family Support Unit. Are Rebecca and Stephanie Kidd also on board this vessel?"

Yeah. Storm's real name is Stephanie.

"Maybe," said Tommy.

Constable Wilmot lowered his shades again

and arched another eyebrow. "Did you, perchance, leave port without your two sisters?"

"Constable Wilmot," I said, "why, all of a sudden, is our family fishing expedition something for the RCIPS to worry about?"

"We have reason to believe that you, your brother, and your two sisters are currently in the Caymans without adult supervision."

"Yo," said Tommy, "I'm eighteen. In, like, six more months."

"And I hope to be invited to the party." I think that was the constable making a joke. You sometimes can't tell when the joke teller has a British accent. "However, for the next six months, you are a minor in the eyes of the law. Therefore, as both of your parents are deceased—"

"What?" said Beck, climbing up the steps from the cabin to join us on the aft deck. "Who said Mom and Dad are dead?"

Constable Wilmot rocked back on the heels of his shiny black shoes. "Certain interested parties."

"You mean certain interested liars," said Beck,

handing the constable a sheet of paper.

"And what, pray tell, is this?"

"An e-mail from our not-dead dad. He's meeting us back in George Town as soon as we're finished out here with our scuba lessons."

CHAPTER 17

"Scuba lessons?" said Constable Wilmot, taking off his sunglasses so we could all see both of his eyebrows hunching up like skeptical caterpillars.

"That's right," said Beck, because she didn't see me trying to shush her without the police officer seeing me shush her.

"According to your brother, ma'am, you are currently on a deep-sea fishing expedition."

"Well," said Beck, "technically, we, uh…"

"We chase after the fish in our scuba gear," I said. "We use spearguns."

"Fascinating," mumbled Constable Wilmot as

he briskly read the e-mail Beck had just handed him. "This is from your father?"

"That's right," said Beck. "He's back at the dock. Waiting for us."

"Might I inquire as to why this e-mail was sent *from* the same address it was sent *to*?"

"Well, um, you know, the Internet..."

"Actually," I said, "Dad finds it way easier to use only one e-mail address because everything is synced through his cloud. Used to say stuff like, 'Concepts like *from* and *to* are kind of meaningless these days with cloud computing, don't you think?'"

The constable folded up the e-mail and handed it back to Beck. "This e-mail is obviously a forgery." He reached for the radio clipped to his belt. "Jenkins? We have four to escort back to George Town. We'll need to tow their boat into port as well."

"Excuse me?" Storm had made her way back to the stern of the ship. I noticed that the front of her shorts and shirt were sopping wet. "Do you work for the United States of America?"

The constable lowered the radio. "Excuse me?"

Storm pointed to the flag flying from the taffrail at the back of the boat.

"We are flying under the flag of the United States of America," said Storm.

"Be that as it may, miss, you are currently in the jurisdiction of the Royal Cayman Islands Police—"

"I don't think so, sir. While you were interrogating my brothers and sister, it seems we drifted into international waters."

That was why Storm's clothes were soaked!

She'd hoisted our anchor so we could coast farther out to sea.

"As I'm certain you know, constable," Storm continued, "oceans, seas, and waters outside national jurisdictions are referred to as the 'high seas' or, in Latin, *mare liberum*, meaning the 'free sea.'"

"You must be Stephanie," said the constable, looking slightly seasick.

"I prefer to be called Storm, the nickname given to me by my father."

"Now deceased."

I could see dark gray thunderclouds boiling up in Storm's eyes as she glared at Constable Wilmot.

(Yep. That's why Dad gave her the nickname.)

"Officer," she said, sounding like a momma grizzly who's been to law school, "according to the 1982 United Nations Convention on the Law of the Sea, once a vessel is twelve nautical miles out from the baseline of a sovereign coastal state's shores, said vessel falls under the jurisdiction of the nationality of the state whose flag it is entitled to fly."

I smiled. Because I knew Storm was relaying,

word for word, a page she had memorized from that book on maritime law.

"Therefore, since you do not operate under the sovereign authority of the United States of America, you have no jurisdiction over us on the high seas. Kindly leave our vessel."

I felt like singing "God Bless America." Or at least chanting "USA! USA!"

"I am impressed with your knowledge of maritime law," said Constable Wilmot. "However, I beg to differ with your calculation of our current position in relation to—"

Before he could finish, Beck whipped out her digital camera and took a snapshot.

"Young lady," sniffed the constable, "this is hardly the time or place for—"

"Check it out," said Beck, showing the camera's display window to the constable. "It's a GPS camera."

PROPERTY OF THE CAYMAN ISLANDS

LAND OF THE FREE HOME OF THE BRAVE

WE ARE HERE!

I joined in: "According to a whole bunch of satellites that never tell a lie, we are definitely in international waters. And you, Constable Wilmot, need to get off our boat."

The RCIPS officer stared at the tiny screen.

Nodding grimly, he reached for his radio.

"Jenkins? Belay my original orders. Only one to come aboard." He gave Storm a crisp salute off the brim of his cop cap. "Well played, young lady."

Storm saluted back. "Enjoyed sparring with you, Officer."

The constable went back to his police boat, which turned tail and sailed back toward the Caymans.

Meanwhile, on the deck of *The Lost*, we Kidds were locked in a major-league, American-style group hug.

Around Storm.

CHAPTER 18

The first thing Tommy did when he returned to the helm was flip the "silence switch" on our AIS transponder so nobody could track where we were headed.

"Always a wise move," he said with a wink, "in pirate-infested waters."

Or if your ship's movements are being closely monitored by the police from your last port of call. Or maybe Louie Louie.

Let's face it: Somebody had sent the RCIPS boat after us. My money was on our parents' so-called friend. I'd seen how Louie Louie was drooling over the treasure on display in the deckhouse.

He must've figured there was even better loot stashed somewhere down below.

"I'm going into The Room," Storm announced.

"Why?" said Beck.

"Anything I see that looks superimportant, I'm going to temporarily stow in some of the secret compartments. Just in case we have any more unexpected company."

Storm went off to wherever she had last hidden The Key.

"How much longer till we reach the dive site?" asked Beck.

"I guesstimate twelve hours," said Tommy.

"We'll be hauling gold bars out of a shipwreck before we know it!" I cheered.

"But what if there's nothing down there?" said Beck. "What if we come up empty-handed?"

"Yo, chill, Beck," said Tommy. "Talk like that could jinx the dive."

"But I'm serious. We need to find this treasure, or we're sunk."

"Whoa. Bad choice of words, li'l sis. Just chillax. No matter what, we're gonna be golden."

"Promise, Tommy?"

"Promise."

Around eight the next morning, we dropped anchor directly over the spot where the tiny treasure map said we'd find one of the galleons from the lost Córdoba fleet.

(Thanks for drawing the giant *X* on the water, Beck. I've always thought there should be one bobbing up and down in the waves when we reach a treasure site.)

"Gear up!" called Tommy.

Beck, Tommy, and I were already in our wet suits.

Storm, as always, would be staying with the boat. She never went on dives. She couldn't stand the feeling of the snug and rubbery wet suit, and besides, someone had to be on board in case of emergencies.

We dipped our fins into the water to make them easier to pull on and hoisted the heavy air tanks over our shoulders.

I yanked my straps tight across the chest and locked them down. I turned the valve on my tank, jammed the regulator into my mouth, and snapped my mask into place.

Dive leader Tommy sliced into the water like a knife. Beck slipped in right behind him.

I leaped off the deck and plunged into the turquoise-blue water.

It was time to hunt some treasure!

CHAPTER 19

Everything went silent.

I could hear my own breathing but not much else. Beck's swim fins scissor-kicked a few yards ahead of me, creating a swirl of tiny air bubbles that sent neon-bright fish scurrying away in every direction. I raced to catch up with her.

It didn't take long to reach the bottom. The water trapping our sunken treasure ship was maybe forty feet deep. I saw a fish that looked like a snake with fins wiggling above a coral reef colored seven shades of pink. To my left, Tommy was stirring up a murky whirlwind of sand, running a submersible metal detector back and forth across the sea floor.

He shook his head.

Nothing.

Beck was to my right, plunging her metal-detecting probe into the sandy bottom. I followed her lead, poking the ground around me. If we

came upon coins or silver bars or another conquistador helmet, our detectors would start ping-
ing in our ears.

Nothing.

We searched and searched.

For forty-five full minutes.

Our tanks were running dangerously low on
air, and I could tell Beck was as frustrated as
I was.

Suddenly, Tommy signaled that he had found
something.

Beck and I swam over to where he was yanking a squarish object (a sea chest, maybe?) out of
a muddy blur of sand and shells. The thing was
so caked with ocean dreck that there would be
no telling what it was until we cleaned it up. We
helped Tommy shove whatever he had just found
into a catch net, and the three of us kicked our
fins and hauled the bundle, which was very heavy,
up to the surface.

When we finally heaved the net up onto the
deck, it landed with a heavy thud.

Tommy tore his regulator out of his mouth and flipped back his mask. "This is it, you guys! The big one! Boo-yah!"

"That net was so heavy!" shouted Beck.

"Gold always is!" I added enthusiastically.

The three of us clambered up the dive ladder and got to work hosing our treasure off and cleaning it up. Which is when we realized a couple of things.

One, it wasn't Spanish. Two, it wasn't treasure.

It was a small, rotting chair the color of driftwood, with a hole in the seat. Beneath the hole was a rusty bucket with a handle attached.

"It's an old-fashioned potty-training seat," said Storm, who'd wandered over to inspect our find. "You know, guys, I don't think many conquistadors used those. The other conquistadors might've laughed."

Tommy, Beck, and I just stood there, dripping on the deck, staring down at the haul from our first treasure hunt without Dad or Mom.

DAHLIA'S TOITY, it said across the back.

Was this a sign of bad luck to come?

Was our whole treasure-hunting business doomed to end up in the crapper?

At the moment, it sure felt that way.

CHAPTER 20

"Bickford?" said Beck. "Might I see you up at the bow?"

"Of course, Rebecca."

As you can probably tell, our total failure on the dive had put my sister and me in the mood for Twin Tirade No. 427.

"We made a huge mistake!" Beck screamed the instant we were alone in the bow pulpit. "We can't keep hunting treasure without Dad and Mom! We stink!"

"One bad dive doesn't mean we're out of business," I said. "We'll go back down."

"Why? Do you want to find Dahlia's binky, too? Maybe her dirty diapers?"

"No, Rebecca, I want to find the gold from that lost Spanish galleon."

"Hello? Earth to Bickford? Were you even under the same water I was? There is no lost Spanish galleon down there."

"Yes, there is!"

"Really? How many conquistadors were named Dahlia?"

"If the lost galleon isn't down there," I shouted, "why did someone draw a map saying it was?"

"Because they're stupid...uh...stupidheads."

(Yes, as noted earlier, Beck often struggles to express herself verbally. So, she tries to make up for it with her drawings.)

Oh, come on. Is that really necessary? What would Dahlia say if she saw what you did with her toity?

BiCK's KICKIN' NEW LiD.

HEh.

"We need to find that treasure," I insisted.

"No, Bick, we need to face facts. Our treasure-hunting days are over. They have been ever since Dad drowned."

"Dad did not drown! He isn't dead!"

"Well, we sure are."

"No, we're not."

"Yes, we are. We have to give up this stupid family business, once and for all."

That hurt. "Really?"

"Maybe."

"Wow."

"That would stink, wouldn't it?"

"Totally."

This was probably our fastest cooldown ever.

Beck pouted. "I don't want to go to real school. All they have to draw with are crayons and finger paints. No charcoals or fine-tipped pens. Some schools don't even have art classes!"

I was getting really sick of Beck's bad attitude, but her rant gave me an idea. "Beck—that's it! A fine-tipped pen...We could have botched the map transfer!"

"What?"

"What if we did something wrong when we copied the tiny treasure map onto the chart? Think about it—that thing is the size of a postage stamp.

A thick-tipped pen could have put us a millimeter off here or there, and we ended up in the totally wrong spot."

"You're right! We just have to study that tiny map much more carefully."

"Come on," I said. "Storm still has it. We'll ask her to chart it again."

"Maybe we should scan it into the computer!" said Beck as we dashed along the sides of the ship, hanging on to the railings the whole way. The wind was whipping along pretty fiercely, buffeting and billowing our sails. "Then we can lay it up against the digital charts in our navigational app."

"Excellent suggestion, Rebecca!"

"Why, thank you, Bickford."

We reached the stern and saw Storm crawling around on her hands and knees searching for something. Tommy was up in the wheelhouse.

"Storm?" I said.

"I was studying the tiny treasure map because maybe I made a mistake when I drew up the chart, and the wind whipped up, and—"

She stopped.

"I am so sorry."

Tears were streaming down both her cheeks.

That gusty wind?

It had given our tiny treasure map a hasty burial at sea.

CHAPTER 21

I think if Storm weren't our sister, Beck and I would have thrown *her* overboard, too.

But she *is* our sister, so we love her all the more for being, well, Storm.

So that night we tried to forget how Storm just completely ruined our lives, and we tried really hard to love her again.

"Accidents happen," I said.

"Usually when I'm around," Storm said, moping.

My sisters and I were down in the girls' cabin.

Storm was sitting on the edge of the lower bunk, staring at her knees and sobbing.

And saying "I'm sorry" a lot.

"I am so, so sorry, you guys. Seriously. You have no idea how sorry I am."

"Well," said Beck, "we are where we are. There's nothing we can do to change what happened."

"Yeah," I said, trying to dismiss our latest disaster as if it were no big deal. "So we lost a treasure map. At least we still have each other."

Okay. I knew it sounded cornier than the worst greeting card on the sappy rack. But I had to say something.

Storm looked up. Instead of thunderclouds and lightning bolts in her eyes, all I saw was a dull sadness.

"That's just it. You three are stuck with me. I'm no good for anything. I won't dive. I'm no help running the sails or working the rigging. Let's be honest, I'm nothing but a bloated blob of ballast. A lump of deadweight that's dragging the rest of you guys down."

"Actually," said Tommy, who'd made a surprise appearance in the hallway outside Storm and Beck's cabin door, "as you know better than anybody, Storm, because you totally memorized the whole nautical-terminology entry on Wikipedia, ballast is something placed on a vessel to, um... what was it again?"

Storm couldn't help but fill in the blank for Tommy: "Provide desired stability."

"Yeah, that's what I was gonna say. Ballast on, like, a balloon, can, um..."

Storm smiled a little. "Control the center of gravity."

"Exactly," said Tommy. "You're our rock, Storm. In a good way. Not like, you know, gravel. Or a rock in your shoe."

"You're like the Rock of Gibraltar," I said. "You're the rock-solid center that helps the rest of us stay on course."

"Thanks, you guys," Storm mumbled. "But—"

"But nothing," said Beck. "Who outsmarted that Cayman Islands cop yesterday?"

"And who busted Daphne, the mask thief?" I added.

Now Storm couldn't help but grin. She raised her hand. "That would be me."

"And were you not, on both occasions, totally awesome?" said Tommy. "Besides, if you ask me, that map we were following was pretty sucky. Come on—what kind of pirate draws his treasure map on the back of, like, a movie ticket stub?"

"But what about our financial crisis?" said Storm.

Tommy paused. "So you definitely think we're in a crisis here?"

"Yes, Tommy."

"And would you say it's an emergency-type situation, too?"

Storm nodded.

"Cool," said Tommy.

"Uh, what?" said Beck.

"Well, if Storm has declared a state of emergency, I am free to act. Bick, stand by to hoist anchor."

"Huh?"

"We need to shove off and set sail for the Florida Keys. We're gonna go dig up some Spanish doubloons I know about."

"What?!" Beck, Storm, and I all shrieked together.

Tommy shrugged. "Hey, Dad told me if there ever was an emergency financial crisis and he and Mom weren't around, we should go tap into our college fund. He even showed me how to find it. Cool, huh?"

Nobody said a word. For once, I was speechless. Luckily, I have a bigmouthed twin to help me in these situations.

"You mean you knew where we could go to stock up on treasures all this time, and you waited until *now* to say something?" Beck said incredulously.

"I waited until Storm said it was a financial emergency," Tommy explained. "That's what Dad told me to do because he trusted her to know when it was time for a last resort. She's our, you know,

150

compass or whatever. She tells us which way to go."

Storm stood up. "Dad said that about me?"

Tommy nodded. "We couldn't do this without you, Storm. You're as important as any of us. And don't you forget it."

CHAPTER 22

"We need to be in The Room," said Tommy. Storm raced off to the galley. When she came back, she smelled like coffee beans and brown dust was all over her right hand.

Guess we know where she hid The Key that time.

Tommy opened the solid steel door, and the four of us trooped into The Room together.

"Um, what happened to that big, old-school map?" asked Beck.

"I hid it," said Storm. "Along with the photographs of the paintings and Al Capone."

"Where?"

"Sorry," said Storm. "That information is classified."

Beck winked. "Good."

Tommy sat down at the desk and fired up Dad's computer. We clustered behind him so we could see the screen.

"Okay, check it out," said Tommy, clicking on a folder labeled KIDS' COLLEGE FUND.

The file opened and listed several documents and image files.

"You know that legend about the four lost galleons from Córdoba's fleet?"

"Sure," I cracked. "One of them was carrying solid-gold potty-training seats."

"Well, that legend isn't completely true."

"Duh," said Beck. "Don't remind us."

"No, I mean there are only *two* ships still missing. Dad already found the other ones."

"No way," I said.

"Way. In fact, he found them twelve years ago, right after you two were born."

Storm raised her hand. "Tommy? How do you know all of this?"

"Dad told me. That time you found The Key for us in the cookie jar. Anyway, right after Mom had Beck and Bick, Dad found these two underwater twins. He told me he considered the incredible coincidence of having twins and discovering twins to be, like, an omen."

Tommy clicked the mouse and an underwater photograph came up. It showed two Spanish galleons lying side by side at the bottom of the sea, their barnacled masts completely intertwined,

almost as if they were spindly skeletons holding hands.

"The one on the left he dubbed *La Hermosa Señorita Rebecca*. The one on the right he called *El Muy Brillante Señor Bickford*. According to the ships' manifests"—he clicked the mouse again and scrolled down a list of incredible treasures— "these two galleons were carrying more than two thousand boxes of gold and silver coins, plus bullion bars, hundreds of ingots of copper, jewelry, religious medals, and junk like vanilla, chocolate, and indigo."

"Uh, Tommy?" said Beck. "Is this why you told me to 'chillax' yesterday? That no matter what happened, we'd be *'golden'*?"

Tailspin Tommy got a sheepish grin on his face. "Yeah. I was kind of goofing on, you know, the word *gold.*"

"And you know how to reach the dive site?" asked Storm.

Tommy slid a flash drive into the computer. "Even better. I just need to copy this navigational file, load it into the computer up in the wheelhouse, and put *The Lost* on autopilot. It's not too far from Alligator Reef, southeast of Upper Matecumbe Key. But it's far enough out that nobody else knows about it."

"Is this for real, Tommy?" I asked, because I couldn't believe we were finally catching a break.

"Yep. By this time tomorrow, I figure, we'll be the richest kids in the world. Except for, you know, that guy in the comic books. Richie Rich."

I raised both my arms over my head and shouted, "Woo-hoo!"

When the navigational file was copied onto the flash drive, the four of us marched out of the room and paraded up to the wheelhouse singing rock songs and sea chanteys like we used to when we went adventuring with Mom and Dad.

Dad particularly enjoyed a good Jimmy Buffett tune. So while Storm hid The Key someplace new, Beck, Tommy, and I launched into a very loud and extremely off-key rendition of "Cheeseburger in Paradise."

It felt like the good old days—you know, six months ago.

But the days to come were looking up. At the very least, I had a pretty great feeling that when we pulled into port after tapping into our college fund, we'd all be able to order as many cheeseburgers as we wanted.

CHAPTER 23

We sailed north by northeast toward the treasure coast of Florida, our spirits buoyed by hope and the crazy anticipation of the dive to come.

A little after noon, Tommy gave the air horn five sharp blasts.

Yes, this was even bigger than the Dolphins winning the Super Bowl.

"Navigational software is making all the right noises!" Tommy hollered from the poop deck. "Gear up!"

Beck and I had been in our rubberized wet suits since breakfast (not a bad way to eat, by the way, especially if you slurp and spill a lot).

Storm was right there with us, helping us strap on our tanks, checking valves, handing out the dive bags, standing by with fresh tanks so we could keep diving all day. But this time, Beck and I didn't have our sticks to poke the ground. Tommy was so confident about Dad's dive coordinates he was going to be the only one toting a metal detector.

"You guys are gonna need your hands free to scoop up all that booty," he said with a wink.

When the three of us were good to go, we actually grabbed hands and jumped into the water together.

You're basically looking at an underwater wall of bubbles after you do that.

Tommy flashed us a series of hand signals— ending with a thumbs-down.

Don't worry—in diving, that's a good thing. It means "descend."

NO, THE OCEAN IS **NOT** MADE OF SPRITE. THOSE ARE OUR BUBBLES.

We slowly made our way to the bottom, waiting for the moment our twin galleons would appear.

A school of five billion tiger-striped silvery fish parted in front of us like curtains opening on a stage.

And there it was—the silhouette of the intertwined masts. We had found Dad's hidden ships,
tucked up against a coral reef. And I know this is
going to sound weird, but, for just a second, I felt
like Dad was right there beside me, patting me
on the shoulder, giving me a big okay hand signal
because we'd done good.

We'd kept the family together.

We'd helped one another through thick and thin and crying over lost treasure maps.

Now it was time to reap our reward.

Tommy led us around a crustacean-encrusted cannon and down through a narrow hatch opening. Dozens of golden fish were swimming beside us, probably curious to see what we found down in the hold of King Philip III of Spain's long-forgotten galleon.

They weren't disappointed.

Tommy flicked on a floodlight, and I could see we were inside a room the length, width, and depth of our entire ship. The heavily timbered chamber was like a warehouse filled with barnacle-covered sea chests (it looked like someone had poured wet concrete over them) stacked one on top of another.

Tommy signaled to me, and we kicked up to a chest at the top of one stack. Then, using our dive knives, we snapped open the brittle lock and loosened the crusty buildup clinging to the latch hasp.

Tommy raised the heavy lid.

You know those ball pits people sometimes have at birthday parties? Picture that, but instead of brightly colored balls, put in gold coins.

Tommy and I ran our gloved hands through the mound of sparkling treasure. There was so much, it dribbled through our fingers like clamshells into a bucket.

I couldn't help it. I did a slow flip, pumping my arms and making a sound like...well...like I was yelling underwater. We were *rich*! We were *beyond* rich!

Beck swam over toting a rusty old helmet she'd just found. Then the three of us manned our scoops and started filling up bags and buckets and even the helmet with loads and loads of solid gold doubloons.

We made a total of seven dives down to the shipwreck.

While we were hauling everything up, Storm was in charge of counting the coins and sorting them into cloth sacks—the thick kind they carry on armored cars that drop money off at the bank. She put the jewels (diamonds, emeralds, rubies) in separate sacks and kept the artifacts in another pile for further study.

Before the sun had set, we had several million dollars' worth of loot on board *The Lost*.

We didn't feel so lost anymore.

And the two galleons down below?

Tommy said there was no need to be greedy. That it would be smart to keep our "rainy day" bank account open, in case we ever needed to come back and make another withdrawal.

Judging from the treasure I had seen in the cargo hold of that one galleon, that wasn't going to happen anytime soon. The four of us would be able to go to any college we chose, if we wanted to go to college. We could probably buy the football team a new stadium, too.

Tommy was right. We were suddenly the richest kids to ever sail the seven seas!

PART 2

THE PIRATE KING'S TREASURE MAP

CHAPTER 24

There's really only one problem with having ten dozen sacks of antique gold doubloons: You can't really take them to a Coinstar machine

at the supermarket to turn them into modern American cash.

So I made a suggestion: "We should call Louie Louie."

Beck made one of her famous "gag-me-now" finger-throat gestures.

"Seriously," I said. "Look, I know the guy is sleazy. But he knows people who deal with things like this."

"Bick could be right," said Storm. "After all, we haven't fully complied with all the laws of salvages and finds as established under the UN Law of the Sea."

In other words, we weren't all the way to sleazy with our retrieval of the loot, but we were definitely borderline skeevy.

"We should call the creep," Storm said bluntly. "Dad has a satellite telephone in The Room."

"He does?" said Tommy. "Awesome. You guys make the call; I'll steer us out of here. Don't want to draw any undue attention to our secret fishing hole."

Beck and I followed Storm into the head (that's boat talk for bathroom) off Mom and Dad's cabin.

The Key was taped underneath the toilet lid.

Then we headed into The Room, and Storm gestured toward the satellite phone, which was acting as a paperweight on a stack of file folders.

"Now we just need to find Louie Louie's phone number," I said.

"Um, it's in here," said Beck, studying the face of the phone.

"What?"

"Louie Louie. Cayman Islands, three-four-five area code. It was the last call Dad made before he, you know..."

"Disappeared," I said, so Beck and Storm couldn't say "died."

Beck pushed the recall-last-number button and switched on the speakerphone.

"Hello, this is Louie. How may I be of assistance?"

Beck motioned for me to do the talking.

"Uh, Mr. Louie, this is Bick Kidd."

"Really? My, my, my. What a delightful surprise. To what do I owe the pleasure of this call? Are you seeking a buyer for your, shall we say, cargo?"

"No, sir. We have a question."

"Indeed? Do go on."

"Let's say we went for a dive and found some, you know, 'merchandise.' Where would be a good place to take it for a fair...uh...exchange?"

There was a long silence.

"You found merchandise?"

"Yes, sir."

"Recently?"

"Yes, sir. This afternoon."

"Really? My, my, my. Will wonders never cease? Congratulations. Your father and mother would be very proud. Very proud, indeed. Now, then, where are you currently located?"

"Um, that's kind of confidential."

"I see. Of course. Completely understandable. However, if I am to direct you to a merchandise... dealer...I need an approximate geographic location."

Beck mouthed the word *Miami*.

That was good. Miami was about ninety miles north of our secret treasure trove.

"Miami," I said.

"Ah! Good. I have an associate in Miami. A businesswoman interested in doing business with those interested in doing business with her."

"Good. Where do we find this friend?"

"I will make all the arrangements. Simply call me when you reach port, and I will provide you with further instructions."

"Thank you, sir."

"Of course, my finder's fee is fifteen percent."

"But *we* found the treasure."

"And I found the dealer. If my terms are in any way unacceptable..."

I checked out my chief negotiator, Beck. She didn't like it, but she was nodding. Storm, on the other hand, wasn't really paying attention to the phone conversation. She was busy flipping through papers in a manila folder.

"Okay," I said, "you get fifteen percent."

"And, of course, my friend will be entitled to her cut as well."

Beck nodded again.

"Fine. We'll call you when we reach Miami."

"Might I suggest you dock at the Sea Spray Marina?"

"Not if it costs us another fifteen percent!"

"Oh, no, dear boy. The marina already pays me a very handsome retainer fee for all referrals."

"Great. We'll call you when we dock in Miami."

I punched the Off button.

"Yuck," said Beck, shivering. "My ears feel slimy just from listening to him."

"Yeah. He kind of oozes out of the phone."

"And he oozed into here, too," said Storm, tapping the file folder. "According to Dad's notes, Louie Louie holds the key—to *everything*."

CHAPTER 25

S torm showed us the note (scrawled in Dad's handwriting) that she'd just found inside the manila folder:

"Who's Dr. Lewis?" said Beck.

"An expert on antiquities," said Storm, who, apparently, had memorized the latest edition of *Who's Who in Expertise*. "With Mom out of the picture, Professor Lewis was probably the only person Dad trusted to authenticate the bee amulet. He teaches at Columbia University in New York City."

"We should take him the pendant," said Beck.

"Or take it to Mom, over in Cyprus," I suggested.

"You guys?" said Tommy, appearing in the doorway. "First things first. Let's go cash in our treasure."

We docked in Miami at the marina suggested by Louie Louie. He then directed us to a shady character named Miss Laticia, who, it turned out, was a full-service black marketer with a soft spot for orphans.

"Ever since I read that Dickens book!" she wheezed in her froggy voice between coughing fits.

The lady smoked a lot.

Storm had memorized the price of gold on the

mercantile exchanges that morning, so we knew Miss Laticia was giving us a fair price for our doubloons (minus the 30 percent handling fee she split with Louie Louie). Miss Laticia then wire-transferred our profits into a "Kidd Family Trust" bank account she'd set up for us—complete with debit cards that Tommy tested around the corner at the nearest ATM before we officially closed the deal.

Then, never asking any questions as to where or how we found our treasure, Miss Laticia called a stretch limousine and sent us on our way with a briefcase filled with one-hundred-dollar bills.

"I figure you kids could use some 'walking around' money to go with your new, multimillion-dollar trust fund!" She hacked out a laugh that made the two-inch-long ash tube at the tip of her cigarette fall off.

With our money worries officially over, the four of us piled into the back of a very swanky stretch limousine.

"Where to?" asked the driver.

"New York," said Beck.

I countered with "Cyprus."

"Hang on, you guys," said Tommy. "I'm starving."

"Me, too," said Storm.

Now that they mentioned it, Beck and I both agreed that food would be an excellent first investment.

"Who makes the best cheeseburgers in Miami?" I asked.

"Easy," said the driver. "Cheeseburger Baby in South Beach."

So that was where we went, singing "Cheeseburger in Paradise" through the open sunroof the whole way.

CHAPTER 26

T he neon in the window at Cheeseburger Baby
said, YO! WE'RE OPEN.

We hurried in and grabbed stools at the coun-
ter. We were so hungry, everybody—including the
limo driver, who hadn't had lunch and was happy
to hear we were treating—ordered the one-pound
double cheeseburger. Tommy, being the eating
machine that he is, had considered going with
the Punisher, a *five-pound* burger. If you finish
it, you get a free T-shirt and your picture in the
Cheeseburger Baby Hall of Fame.

"The T-shirt wouldn't look good over a bloated
beef belly," he decided.

Storm had a side of cheddar cheese fries with a side of chili cheese fries. Beck and I went with the onion rings.

And we all had root beer floats.

Several of them. This led to a lot of happy burping, which, of course, attracted a lot of attention, including the giggles of several attractive girls. They admired Tommy's "appetite." I think he admired their bathing suits.

So he decided to treat them to milk shakes.

And their friends.

And their friends' friends.

Before long, we were buying everybody in the restaurant—including a couple of beefy guys with handlebar mustaches and a girl in sunglasses who might've been Beyoncé—thick and creamy shakes.

Finally, we settled our tab with four of our crisp one-hundred-dollar bills and slipped another Benjamin (Tommy told me that's the cool way to say "one-hundred-dollar bill") on the counter-top to tip the grill guys, waitstaff, and shake makers. Stuffed, we waddled out to our waiting limo.

"That was fun," I said, stretching out in the backseat and letting loose with a five-second sonic-boom belch. "But now we need to seriously discuss what we're going to do with our money."

"Invest it," said Storm. "I'm pretty good on E-Trade."

"Come back here tomorrow," said Tommy. "Some of those girls wrote their phone numbers on napkins."

"Complete Dad's plan," said Beck. "We sail on to New York."

"No," I said. "We need to head back to Cyprus and rescue Mom."

And that was the start of Twin Tirade No. 428.

I think it was one of our longest. It was definitely one of our loudest and most public—right in front of Storm and Tommy, who tried to ignore us by staring out the limo's tinted windows at all the palm trees rolling by. The driver turned up his radio to drown us out.

"Mom's dead!" screamed Beck.

"No, she's not!" I screamed back.

"You're a dreamer, Bickford."

"So? Without dreams, what've you got?"

"A note from Dad that says 'go to New York,' idiot!"

The tirade continued the entire drive from South Beach back to the marina.

It *kept* going while Storm paid the driver and Tommy shook his head and rolled his eyes.

In fact, Beck and I were still Twin Tirading

all the way up the jetty and out to the berth where we had docked *The Lost*.

We only stopped when a man in mirrored sunglasses stepped out of the deckhouse on *our* boat and shouted, "Rebecca? Bickford? Knock it off. You two are giving me a headache!"

CHAPTER 27

The man in the mirrored sunglasses—who started jabbering into one of those Bluetooth earpieces that made him look like he should be on *Star Trek*—was our Uncle Timothy.

SURGICALLY ATTACHED BLUETOOTH →

WEIRD UNCLE TIMOTHY

He's not really our uncle; he is (or was?) Dad's best friend.

"Expedite the extraction," I heard him say to nobody, which meant he was saying it to whoever was in his ear.

By the way, I have never seen Uncle Timothy without his shades or a cell-phone accessory jammed against his head. I think they're both surgically attached to his skull.

"The assets are in position," he said. "Extract the package at twenty-three hundred hours. You are good to go."

Uncle Timothy was always saying junk like that to someone. For a long time, I thought maybe he worked for UPS or FedEx.

"How are you guys holding up?" he asked.

None of us answered him because we thought he was still talking to his Bluetooth.

"Thomas?"

"Hmm?"

"How are you kids doing?"

Tommy patted his tummy. "Little full right now, Uncle Tim, but, you know, hanging in."

"Well, don't you guys worry. I heard what

happened to your dad. I'm here to take over for him on *The Lost.*"

"Um, Uncle Timothy?" I said.

"Yeah, Bick?"

"How'd you 'hear' about Dad?"

"Hang on." He put two fingers to his Bluetooth. "Well, check the weather forecast again. Clouds move in at twenty-two-thirty. The low ceiling will block out the full moon, so the drop zone will be dark. Follow the protocol. Extract the package. I don't remember exactly where I heard about it, Bick. I just did."

I guessed he was talking to me again. Which made me wonder if I was supposed to go pick up a package for him.

"Uh, well," I said, "it's just kind of interesting that you know about Dad's disappearance when we haven't really told anybody about it."

"But," said Beck, sounding suspicious, "everybody seems to know about it. You, Louie Louie..."

"Did he have the amulet?" said Uncle Timothy.

"Dad?" I said.

"No. Louie Louie."

"Yeah," said Tommy. "Louie had it. But we traded a mask for it."

"Good. The mask is meaningless. The bee is key."

"Totally," said Tommy. "I guess. Not really sure what that means or why everybody keeps saying it—"

"What's in the briefcase?" said Uncle Timothy, quickly shifting gears and gesturing at the aluminum attaché case Storm was hugging to her chest with both arms.

"Oh, that's—" Tommy started.

I cut him off. "Our new tool kit. Keeps everything organized in tidy slots. Hammer, screwdrivers, wrenches, a whole set of those angled things nobody ever uses. Well, Uncle Tim, it was great to see you again."

"And," said Beck, "if we need help, we'll definitely be in touch."

"Hey," I said, "maybe you should give us your cell number."

"No need, Bickford. I'm staying on board *The Lost.*"

"Why?" said Storm bluntly. "We're doing fine. We don't really need your help,"

"Yes, Stephanie. You do. Your father designated me as your legal guardian in the event of a disaster, and I think him falling into the ocean during a tropical storm and drowning qualifies. How about you?"

I was about to say "Dad isn't dead" when Uncle Timothy whipped out a stack of four official-looking documents. They all had GUARDIANSHIP AFFIDAVIT printed across the top, the words bracketed by the official state seal of Florida.

The forms listed our names, dates of birth, and Social Security numbers. They were also signed, sworn to, and notarized. They could have been forgeries, but if they were fakes, they were good ones.

"So, what do you guys want to do for dinner tonight? Maybe head into South Beach and grab some cheeseburgers?"

Ugh. Chowing with Uncle Timothy was the last thing I wanted—except for him taking over *The Lost*.

But it looked like we had no choice.

Uncle Timothy was staying.

CHAPTER 28

The next morning, Tommy and I went through our presail checklist—we disconnected the shore power cord from the dock pedestal, tied down the jib sheets, attached the mainsail halyard shackle, and did about forty other things we do every time we shove off.

We had taken a late-night family vote while Uncle Timothy was pacing around the poop deck jabbering into his cell phone about "dry cleaning," "blowback," and "chicken feed" (I figured he was chatting with a farmer who'd had an unfortunate accident in his chicken coop and needed to get his overalls professionally laundered) and decided that we would use our flush bank account to follow Dad's mysterious instructions and head up to New York City so Professor Lewis could authenticate the Minoan bee amulet. We would not be hopping on the next flight to Cyprus to rescue Mom.

We told Uncle Timothy about our plans to head north.

We did not tell him about the cash in the brief-case.

Then, around 10 AM, we learned why it doesn't always pay to treat people to chocolate milk shakes.

While Tommy and I were prepping *The Lost*, two Miami police officers, both with handlebar mustaches, showed up at our berth. That's right. The same two handlebar-mustached dudes from Cheeseburger Baby.

"Belay that line, son," said the one as he climbed aboard *The Lost*.

"We need to talk to you," said the other, as he boarded behind his partner.

"Uh, hi, guys," I said. "What's up?"

"Why don't you tell us?" said the one.

"Then we'll all know," said the other.

"You kids were flashing a lot of cash yesterday."

"Too much for kids your age."

"Where'd you come up with that kind of money?"

"Are you running drugs on this vessel?"

They kept badgering Tommy and me, hammering us with questions, never really giving us a chance to answer.

"Maybe you two and your sisters need to spend a night as our guests," said the one.

"In the Miami-Dade Juvenile Detention Center," said the other.

"Or we could ship you straight into foster care."

"Or an orphanage."

"Cheeseburgers aren't very good in an orphanage."

"Neither are the onion rings."

That's when Uncle Timothy, trailed by Beck and Storm, stepped out of the deckhouse.

"Good morning, officers. Are my sons in some kind of trouble?"

"Your sons?"

"That's right." Uncle Timothy shot out his arm to shake hands with the police officers. "I'm Timothy Kidd. These are my sons, Thomas and Bickford. My lovely daughters, Stephanie and Rebecca."

"Well, maybe you can answer a few questions for us."

"I'll try," said Uncle Timothy, adjusting his mirrored sunglasses.

"Where did your kids come up with enough

cash to buy everybody in Cheeseburger Baby a milk shake?" said the one.

"And fries," said the other. "I had fries, too."

"Easy. I give my children a very generous allowance. I suppose I spoil them. But, you see, ever since their mother died, well..."

Uncle Timothy acted like the memory of our dead mom was choking him up.

"Excuse me, officers. I don't mean to weep like this. It's just that you've stirred up some very painful memories. We...all...miss...her...so...much...BWAAAAAAH!"

Uncle Timothy started blubbering. The two officers began backing up.

"That's okay, Mr. Kidd."

"Sorry for the intrusion."

"Our condolences on your loss."

"And, uh, thanks, kids. For the milk shakes."

Then they basically ran out of the marina.

When they were gone, Uncle Timothy touched his Bluetooth earpiece and wandered back into the deckhouse. "Sorry about that, Dieter. Family emergency. Call Paris. Contact the DGSE...."

"Okay," said Beck, when he was gone. "I guess we owe the guy one."

We all nodded. He hadn't even asked us about the cash the cops said we were flashing.

But he'd known about our dad going overboard without our telling him.

So there was really no way to be sure: *Was Uncle Timothy a good guy or a bad guy?*

CHAPTER 29

B efore we got a chance to figure out what was really up with Uncle Timothy, he received another cell phone call that sent him tearing out of Miami in a sleek silver craft that looked more like an aerodynamic spaceship than a motorboat.

As he was packing up his things, he said, "Sorry, kids, I have urgent business to attend to. But remember: Your father is counting on you to take care of *his* urgent business. Follow the plan he laid out for you. Take this thing all the way to New York!"

We set sail about twenty minutes later, just the four of us again. But an hour out of port, I was kind of wishing Uncle Timothy were still on board pretending to be our father.

Because three very menacing skiffs had appeared on the horizon.

Tommy raised his binoculars. "They don't look very friendly."

They also looked like they had outboard racing motors attached to the squared-off sterns of their flat-bottomed hulls.

"I count three men in two of the boats, two in the other," said Tommy.

TROUBLE!

"Are they pirates?" asked Beck.

"They look more like surfer dudes," said Tommy, lowering his binocs.

As if he was trying to prove Tommy wrong, one of the guys in the second boat stood up and started waving a red Jolly Roger flag—emblazoned with a football. I think he'd bought it at a Tampa Bay Bucs souvenir shop.

"We need more speed," Tommy barked. "Pull down on the boom and stretch the mainsail. Lose that twist up at the top."

"Aye, aye!" Beck and I scampered up on top of the deckhouse to deal with the mainsail.

When we'd made the adjustments, *The Lost* definitely picked up speed.

"I want the wind coming at us from the side!" Tommy shouted as he yanked the wheel hard to port. "Storm? Set my sails forty-five degrees to the wind!"

Storm did some lightning-fast trigonometry in her head and started calling out vectors and tacks for Tommy to take to put our sails in primo position.

Soon we were clipping along at twice the speed of the wind.

But even the swiftest sailboats have a top speed. The faster we flew, the longer the waves alongside our hull grew. Finally, we passed our limit, what they call hull speed, and it was like we were sailing uphill, fighting our own wake.

In no time, one of the skiffs was right behind

us. The other two were coming alongside our port and starboard.

"Slack your mainsail!" screamed the man standing in the bow of the boat directly behind us. "Or I'll slack it for you!"

He was gripping the wooden stock of a battered machine gun and had bandoliers of bullets draped across his chest.

Two grappling hooks came swinging over the sides and caught hold on our handrails.

"Slack that sail, duder!" The man behind us blasted a quick burst of machine-gun fire into the air.

"Slack the sail, Bick," Tommy called out. "Beck, cast off the headsail sheet. Let it fly!"

We did as Tommy said. *The Lost* dumped all the wind in its sails and swung sideways like a weather vane, our bow ending up pointing in the direction that the wind was blowing. We basically stopped on a dime and dragged those two hooked-on pirate skiffs with us.

The guy with the machine gun—a tattooed surfer dude with long, greasy hair and a hipster

chin beard—hopped onto our stern. His seven surfer dude buddies boarded after him.

"Bodacious sailing, hotdogger," the pirate leader said to Tommy up in the wheelhouse as his scurvy pals swarmed down the sides of our ship, sliding all sorts of clacking levers to rack fresh rounds into their weapons. They all looked like tanned rejects from a biker bar.

"But now, Skipper Dipper," the pirate leader continued, "you need to take a chill pill, dig?"

Tommy just stood in the wheelhouse, glaring down at the cluster of nasty pirates and shielding Storm, who had slid behind him for cover. Beck and I held our position on top of the deckhouse. For a second, I thought about swinging out the boom arm and bowling over some of the thugs. But I'd only be able to hit half of them before the other half opened fire with their wicked assortment of weapons.

"Chillax, little duders. We don't want any of your conquistador helmets or coconut heads."

His friends all chuckled.

"We just want what's in The Room."

CHAPTER 30

"**C**ome on, *mis amigos*," yelled the pirate captain. "We need to be downstairs."

Beck and I glanced at each other. Our eyes were asking the same question: *How could these gnarly surfer pirates know about The Room?*

The eight jangling surfer hoods scampered into the deckhouse. This was really weird. They didn't even leave somebody to guard us. Hey, if you have to get your ship invaded by pirates, I highly recommend the dumb surfer kind!

"Tommy?" I called out.

"Let's roll," he said. "Beck? Stick with Storm."

"On it."

Tommy and I slid down the ladder from the poop

deck and bolted into the deckhouse. Amazingly, none of the pirates were plundering any of the treasure on display in the salon, except one short headbanger with a ponytail who was trying on the conquistador helmet.

Tommy and I hurried down into the hull.

The pirate leader was pounding on the steel door to The Room.

Then a couple of his goons tried prying the door open with the muzzles of their rifles. After a lot of grunting and groaning, five of them started

kicking the door—never a particularly bright move when you're wearing water socks.

"Okay, Skipper Dipper," the red-faced leader said to Tommy. "Where's the freaking key?"

Tommy shrugged. "Don't know."

"Our Dad had it when he fell overboard," I added.

"What?" said the pirate boss.

"Well, you see, there was this storm. The sky darkened. The wind came whipping up out of the west. 'Lie ahull, laddies!' Dad cried from the wheelhouse, as he fought with the wheel to keep us from capsizing. I was up in the crow's nest, my shirt shredded into tatters by the howling, gale-force winds…"

The pirate goons were hanging on my every word.

Except the boss guy.

He racked back the bolt on his machine gun. "The key, kid. Where is it?"

"At the bottom of the sea," I said, trying to fake-sob the way Uncle Timothy did. "In Davy Jones's locker with dear old Dad. BWAAAAH!"

"Quit crying, kid. Where's the spare?"

"There isn't one."

"What?"

"Our dad, may he rest in peace, was kind of cheap. Bought all his shirts at Kmart. And keys for that lock cost, like, ten bucks each. You have to see a locksmith. You can't just go to the nearest Ace Hardware and—"

"Trash the boat!" yelled the pirate leader.

"Woo-hoo!" his rowdy friends shouted in reply.

Suddenly, sheets and blankets were being yanked off our bunk beds. Pillows were flying. Somebody stuffed a coconut head in a commode and flushed it, flooding the floor. Everything that wasn't bolted down or nailed to the walls was knocked over, kicked, dinged, and totally trashed. They even smashed the glass of our *Titanic* steak knife display case. The little guy with the pony-tail drop-kicked the conquistador helmet across the parlor at his buddy, who was slashing our string of jalapeño pepper party lights.

I looked to Tommy.

"It's just stuff," he mumbled. "Let it go."

Fortunately, we had already traded all our gold doubloons with Miss Laticia, and Storm had been clever enough to stash our aluminum suitcase full of cash in one of *The Lost*'s many hidey-holes.

The pirate leader stuck two fingers in his mouth and whistled.

"Playtime's over, dudes. We need to report back to the man. Let's grab the backup package and boogie."

The thieves scampered out of the cabins and deckhouse and started firing their weapons into the air like Yosemite Sam.

"Stay here!" Tommy yelled, racing after the pirates.

Yeah, right.

I charged up the stairs after him, but I could hear the pirates' skiff motors already firing up.

We found Storm still up in the wheelhouse, but now she was crying like crazy.

"What's wrong?" I hollered. "Where's Beck?"

"The pirates! They took her!"

That's when it hit me: Beck was their "backup package."

CHAPTER 31

I'd never felt so sick in my life.

I had the chills. Then I was burning up with fever. I was even throwing up over the side of the boat.

Yes, I was seasick, even though the boat wasn't moving.

Tommy had decided to drop anchor and work the radio. He'd alerted the Coast Guard to the kidnapping. He'd asked our new friends at the Miami PD to issue an all-points bulletin and an Amber Alert.

Meanwhile, Storm was in The Room, running through an FBI database on the web, trying to match the pirate faces she had recently memorized with mug shots on a known-felon list.

I guessed Tommy would've called Uncle Timothy, too, but Uncle Timothy had never given us his cell phone number.

Me?

I was basically useless.

I spent several hours hugging a railing up in the bow pulpit. Moaning. Groaning. Puking.

It was like someone had sawed me in half.

(Yeah, I'm kind of waiting for Beck to draw a picture of that: me split in two. Maybe by a crazed pirate magician with a chain saw. But Beck isn't here to see what a wreck I am, so she can't draw me.)

Losing my twin sister is the worst thing to ever happen to me, because we've been together our whole lives. Think about it. We were together *before* we were even born.

This was worse than losing Mom and Dad.

Beck, of course, would violently disagree with that.

So, since she wasn't there, I had Twin Tirade No. 429—with myself.

"Don't be ridiculous, Bickford!" I shouted, pitching my voice slightly higher, so I sounded like Beck. "How can losing one person be worse than losing two?"

"Um, hello? I've known you nine months longer than I knew either of them."

"Right. Those first nine months were *so* exciting—"

"They were! Remember how we used to kick Mom in the stomach?"

"That was your idea, Bickford."

"You did it, too, Rebecca."

"Because you have always been a bad influence on me."

"Me? What about you?"

"I never made you do anything stupid, Bick."

"What about that time I ate a booger?"

"That was your idea, boogerhead."

"It was not!"

"Was too."

"Wasn't."

"Was!"

"Oh. You're right. It was."

"Yeah. Sorry."

"My bad."

"No worries. We're cool."

I took a pause from yelling at myself.

"So, Bick?" I asked in my Beck voice.

"Yeah, Beck?"

"How'd that booger taste?"

I didn't answer.

I just leaned out over the side of the boat and hurled again.

CHAPTER 32

S o this is me, four hours after the pirates struck.

WARNING: PICTURES BELOW AT KINDERGARTEN ART LEVEL ☹

← THE LOST

ME

← BARF

(For the record, I have, in Beck's absence, taken over the drawings. It might be a little hard to tell us apart. Tommy will no longer have a buff bod. Or cool hair. I apologize.)

It took about eight more hours for Tommy and Storm to finally shake me out of my state of shock.

"Come on, little bro," said Tommy. "Snap out of it!"

"We need you, Bick," said Storm. "Beck wouldn't want you to be this sad."

"You guys are right. I need to pull myself together!"

(Man, how I wish Beck were here to draw a picture of that! Me pulling myself together. Maybe screwing my head onto my butt; putting my feet where my hands should be. For now, you'll just have to use your imagination. Thanks.)

Anyway, I was trying to stay optimistic. But

it was hard. Especially when the sun started to set and Storm and Tommy started talking about Beck as if she were dead, too.

"You know, I'll miss how she used to do those drawings of the seagulls and fish," said Storm. "She didn't need a photographic memory to get every detail just right."

"Remember her first painting?" said Tommy with a chuckle.

"Yeah," said Storm. "That finger-painting number on the walls of the nursery. She used a jar of baby food. Creamed spinach. Mom and Dad called it her 'green period.'"

"Yeah," said Tommy, remembering the scene. "But I swear, she totally nailed Oscar the Grouch."

"Um, you guys?" I said. "Are we having another funeral at sea here?"

"Nah," said Tommy. "We're just, you know, thinking about Beck."

"You want me to run down to the cabin and grab her Marlins cap?" blurted Storm. "We could toss it into the ocean like we did with Dad's captain hat."

"You guys?" I said. "Come on. You're freaking me out. Beck is not dead."

Tommy draped his arm over my shoulder. "And she never will be, bro. Not as long as we keep her here." He tapped his heart.

Man, I thought, *could this get any worse?*

And then, of course, it did.

I heard the whine of a motorboat in the distance. And it didn't sound like the pirates' skiffs.

Now what?

CHAPTER 33

Amazingly, some good news came sailing our way.

The boat emerging out of the sunset and gunning for us—its bow skimming across the waves like a side-armed skip stone—was Uncle Timothy's aerodynamic speedboat. Uncle Timothy was at the wheel.

And Beck was standing at his side.

Her 3-D glasses were strapped on tight, both arms held up high, hair blowing in the breeze. She screamed, "Cowabunga!" as the sleek silver boat bounded across the rolling ocean like a rocket ship.

(As you can see, Beck skipped the tears, hugging, and other mushy junk that happened when we were all reunited on the deck of *The Lost*. Instead, she went with the action scene. Yes, Beck. It was a superawesome entrance, and you looked totally cool. Good call.)

"Uncle Timothy rescued me!" Beck said excitedly. "And get this, you guys: They have a submarine!"

"Who?" I said.

"The pirates! I didn't see it, because they kept me blindfolded the whole time, but I heard them say stuff like 'Tie off to the submarine' and 'Take her down into the submarine,' which, if they wanted to keep the submarine a secret, was totally stupid."

"Didn't the blindfold crush your 3-D glasses?" asked Storm, who I think was tired of seeing Beck wear them.

"Nah. They told me to take them off before they did the whole blindfold bit."

"And you rescued her?" Tommy said to Uncle Timothy.

"Let's just say I negotiated her release. They're pirates. All they want is money—from stolen goods or ransom fees. It makes no difference to scum like that."

"How much did I cost?" asked Beck. "Was it, like, a million bucks?"

Uncle Timothy grinned. "We came to terms."

"Well, I'm glad you did!"

"Me too," I said, feeling whole again, now

that Beck was safe. "Did they hurt you?"

"No. They just kept asking me a bunch of questions. It was like one of those interrogation scenes in a spy movie. They even hooked me up to a lie detector machine!"

"Really?"

"Yeah. They wrapped this bulky Velcro thing around my wrist and slid my fingers into these electrode cups."

"I thought you were blindfolded," said Storm.

"I was," said Beck. "But the pirates all went 'upstairs' to talk to 'The Man' when they ran out of questions. So I slipped the bandana up real quick and peeked."

"What'd you see?" I asked.

"The lie detector paper with lots of squiggly lines and some other junk. Like an ashtray filled with soggy cigar butts."

I had a feeling Beck might've seen something else but didn't want to say what it was in front of everybody. "What kind of questions were they asking you?"

"Everything! They wanted to know about Dad's most recent treasure hunts and Mom disappearing in Cyprus. Then, get this, they started asking a lot of art questions like 'Have you ever seen Van Gogh's *Poppy Flowers* or Cézanne's *Boy in a Red Waistcoat*?'"

"The photos Dad had down in The Room?"

"Yep."

"What'd you do?"

"I told the truth. I said, 'No, I have never seen those paintings.'"

"But you have," said Storm.

"No. All I've seen are *photographs*, not the paintings!"

"So you beat the machine?" I said.

"Totally," said Beck. "Because I wasn't telling a lie."

At that moment, I was exceptionally proud to be Beck's twin.

"Wait a second," said Tailspin Tommy. "How did those pirates know what pictures Dad had pinned to the walls in The Room? Did they, like, drill a peephole in the door or something?"

"There's no hole in the door," Storm said. "Besides, Dad's photographs of those paintings weren't in The Room when the pirates boarded *The Lost*. I'd hidden them."

"Right," said Tommy. "I forgot that part. I'm glad you remembered."

"So how did they know?" I mumbled. "Not just about the paintings. About Mom and Cyprus. Everything."

Beck turned to Storm. "Here's the worst part. More than anything, they wanted The Key."

"Did you tell them where it was?" asked Tommy, that dizzy tailspin look in his eyes again.

"Um, no. Only Storm knows where it's hidden, remember?"

"Oh. Riiiight. Forgot that part, too."

"Well," said Uncle Timothy, who, if you ask me, had stayed a little too quiet the whole time Beck told us her kidnapping tale, "it seems the pirates shanghaied the wrong daughter. They should've kidnapped Storm."

CHAPTER 34

"They can't have Storm, either!" I said, eye-balling Uncle Timothy pretty hard.

"Just a joke, Bickford. No reason to get all bent out of shape, son."

Actually, there *was* a reason to twist myself into a pretzel: There was something suspicious going on. Something weird about Uncle Timothy.

"So, Uncle Timothy," I said, "thanks for bringing Beck back."

"You're welcome, Bickford."

"Quick question."

"Yes?"

"How did you know where the pirates had taken her?"

I couldn't tell how Uncle Timothy reacted to my question because his eyes were still shielded behind their silver mirrors. Also, nothing on his face budged or twitched. The man might have been chiseled out of marble.

HOW DID HE KNOW WHERE TO FIND ME?

INTERNATIONAL MAN OF MYSTERY

WHAT HAPPENS WHEN HE LOOKS AT HIS MIRRORED SUNGLASSES IN THE MIRROR?

HOW MUCH DOES HE SPEND ON LENS POLISH EVERY YEAR?

"My boat," he finally said, gesturing toward the floating rocket ship tied off to our stern, "is equipped with sophisticated radio scanners. I happened to be monitoring a band of frequencies known to be employed by those in the pirating trade."

I raised my hand.

"Yes, Bickford?" Uncle Timothy sighed.

"Got another question for ya."

"Yes?"

"How come the pirates called Beck the 'backup *package*'?"

"Most likely their initial target was something else. Probably The Key to The Room. They took Beck as a backup."

(Did you notice how he totally avoided explaining why the pirates used the word *package*, a term Uncle Timothy uses all the time? Yeah, me, too.)

"I have a question, too," said Storm.

"My goodness," Uncle Timothy said with a pretty fake chuckle. "This is worse than the grilling those pirates gave Rebecca."

"How did you know where the pirates' submarine was located?"

"I told you. I tracked their radio transmissions."

"No. You said you monitored 'a band of frequencies known to be employed by those in the pirating trade.'"

"Do you have gear on your ship to pinpoint the transmission site, too?" asked Tommy, because he loves cool gadgets.

"Look, kids," said Uncle Timothy. (Quick observation: Whenever a grown-up calls a group of kids "kids," you know they're about to *not* tell you something.) "I can't answer all these questions right now. You just have to trust me."

We all nodded.

But I noticed that my siblings, even Tailspin Tommy, were eyeing Uncle Timothy the way I'd been eyeing him earlier.

Who was this Uncle Timothy who wasn't really our uncle?

Whose side was he really on?

Ours?

The pirates'?

Or was he in league with somebody we hadn't even met yet?

CHAPTER 35

s we sailed north, towing Uncle Timothy's
boat behind us, my suspicions about the mysterious man in the mirrored sunglasses continued
to grow.

By the way, he didn't allow any of us to board
his boat or check out the cool gizmos inside. That
made my doubts grow bigger than mutant, radio-
active tomatoes.

"Something's fishy about Uncle Timothy," I
confided to Beck.

"It's his safari vest," said Beck. "I think he
was gutting tuna before he rescued me."

"I'm serious!"

"I know. And for what it's worth, I think there's something shady about him, too."

"Do you think he found you on the pirates' submarine because he's working with the pirates?"

"It's a possibility. Plus, Dad probably told Uncle Timothy about The Room...."

"...And he told the pirates."

"That's how they knew about the photographs of the paintings...."

"...And what happened to Mom in Cyprus. Family meeting?"

"Yeah," said Beck. "I have an idea. Something I picked up in the pirate submarine."

"Like using a lie detector on him?"

"Something better."

We rounded up Storm and Tommy and had a quick meeting up on the poop deck.

Beck showed us the slender box she had "borrowed" from her pirate captors.

"You stole that?" said Storm.

"Hey, they were going to use it on me. Besides, is it really against the law to steal stuff from people who have nothing on board their boat but stuff they've stolen from other people's boats?"

Tommy nodded thoughtfully. "Wow. That's heavy, Beck."

Just then, Uncle Timothy strolled out of the deckhouse and stretched his arms, taking in the warm sunshine bathing the back end of our boat.

"That's a dumb plan, Bickford!" shouted Beck, shooting me a wink, to let me know Twin Tirade

No. 430 was intended solely for Uncle Timothy's ears.

"Oh, yeah? Well, what's your plan, Rebecca?"

"Easy! We steal those stupid sunglasses he's always wearing and make him sit in the sun!"

"And how's that going to make him tell us the truth?"

"He has sensitive eyes!"

"So? He can close them!"

"Not if we force them open."

"And how are we gonna do that?"

"I have some pliers," Tommy chimed in.

"We have those hot dog tongs, too," added Storm.

"Kids?"

Uncle Timothy, hands on hips, was staring up at us from down below.

"Oh, hey, Uncle Tim," I said. "We didn't know you were down there."

"Obviously. Look, I've told you all that I can, okay? Now knock it off, Bick and Beck." He stretched into a yawn. "I'm bushed. Gonna go grab a quick nap down below. Don't wake me up unless there's another pirate attack."

"Yes, sir," we all said in four-part harmony.

I couldn't believe my eyes: Uncle Timothy actually took the Bluetooth device out of his ear.

He was definitely shutting down for nap time.

"We give him ten minutes to zonk out," whispered Beck when he was gone. She slid the thin box out of her pocket. "Then we give him this."

We all nodded.

Because, like I said earlier, we Kidds are Wild Things.

And even though what we were planning to do to Uncle Timothy was probably illegal (not to mention potentially lethal), we were going to do it anyway.

When cornered, we have no fear of adults and zero interest in obeying the rules of their so-called society.

We'd give Uncle Timothy ten minutes to fall asleep.

Then the Wild Things would pounce.

CHAPTER 36

What Beck had swiped from the pirates' underwater interrogation room was a thin box about the size graduation pen sets come in.

The box was labeled TRUTH SERUM.

I guess that's one way to make sure nobody beats your lie detector: Give them a shot of truth juice.

Under the box's clamped lid were a syringe and a vial of Pentothal—a fast-acting, short-lasting drug that's

YIKES.
THIS IS SOME
SERIOUS STUFF!

used for all sorts of medical reasons, including numbing the part of the brain that makes up lies.

Storm spent five minutes memorizing everything several Internet nursing sites had on how to safely give an injection. Then the four of us tiptoed into the main cabin, where Uncle Timothy was sacked out on the bed.

"Sorry about this, Uncle Tim," said Storm as she jabbed him in the arm with the needle. "But we need to know the whole truth and nothing but the truth."

Weirdly, Uncle Timothy didn't wake up when Storm stabbed him. He just kind of snorted and shifted, swatting at his arm, then went still again.

We gave the drugs a minute to kick in.

Then Tommy splashed some cold water out of a bottle on Uncle Timothy's face.

"Huh?" he said, waking up.

"Who are you?" I asked.

"Your uncle Timothy."

"But who are you really?"

And Uncle Timothy started talking.

"My name is Timothy Quinn."

"ANYBODY WANT TO PLAY TRUTH OR DARE?"

"Who do you work for? The pirates?"

He shook his head. "No. I work for the Agency. The CIA."

"The Central Intelligence Agency? You're a spy?"

"Affirmative. I organize and orchestrate clandestine operations to keep America safe. Just this week, under the cover of darkness, we extracted several US citizens who were being held hostage in the notorious mountain regions of Pakistan. I'm happy to report that the package was safely delivered without significant blowback."

"What's *blowback*?"

"Unintended consequences of covert activities, such as civilian casualties."

Okay. That was pretty dramatic.

"How do you know Dad?" asked Beck.

"Your father, Thomas Kidd, works for me."

"What?"

"He is, or *was*, a CIA agent."

"Dad worked for you?" I blurted. "Seriously?"

"Yes. So does, or did, your mother."

"Whoa," said Tommy. "Mom's a spy, too?"

"Are Dad and Mom alive?" I demanded, not waiting for the answer to Tommy's question.

"I cannot say at this time."

"Well," said Storm, "are they dead?"

"I do not know."

This gave me hope. "So they might be alive?"

"They are both extremely talented operatives. However, their most recent missions were and remain extremely dangerous. I give them each a thirty percent chance of survival."

I smiled. Hey, 30 percent is way better than "definitely deceased."

If Uncle Timothy was telling the truth (and he didn't really have a choice right now), we might even need to buy Dad a new captain's hat at our next port to replace the one we'd tossed overboard at his funeral.

CHAPTER 37

"What'd you give me, kids?" said Uncle Timothy after the truth serum had worn off. He rubbed his arm where Storm had poked him. "Pentothal?"

"Actually," said Storm, "the drug's generic name is sodium thiopental."

"I know," said Uncle Timothy. "We used to use it. Until something better came along."

"So where exactly is Mom?" I asked. "And Dad?"

"I have no information on their current whereabouts."

"Well, are they dead or alive?"

"Yes."

"That's it?" said Beck. "That's totally lame!"

"And extremely cryptic," I said, using the biggest word I knew for *secretive* and *sneaky*.

Storm tugged on my shirt. "He's a spy. Cryptic is what spies do."

Uncle Timothy touched his Bluetooth earpiece, which he had slipped back on after our truthfest.

(By the way, he even *sleeps* in his sunglasses!)

"Roger that," Uncle Timothy said to whoever was jabbering in his ear. "Tommy? Cut loose my boat."

"What?"

"Cut the line," he barked. "Then put some distance between your vessel and mine."

"Um, okay. Bick?"

"On it."

I went to the cleat where we'd tied off Uncle Timothy's superboat, which, now that we knew the truth about him, I realized was probably some kind of top secret stealth seacraft, the kind that could sneak up on a submarine undetected. With a nod from Uncle Timothy, I cut the rope and ran back to the group.

Tommy was up in the wheelhouse. He fired up

the engines and took us about a hundred yards due west of the spy boat.

"That's good enough for government work," hollered Uncle Timothy.

Tommy cut our engines.

That's when Uncle Timothy tugged one of the zippers on his safari vest, hard.

KA-BOOM!

His high-tech spy boat exploded.

"It was only a prototype," he said coolly, as if that explained how it was all right to blow up a perfectly good bajillion-dollar spy ship. "Still, we can't risk letting the technology fall into the wrong hands."

Tommy was at the poop deck railing, his mouth hanging open, staring at the billowing ball of black smoke where the obliterated boat used to be. "Awesome, dude."

"Thank you, Thomas." Uncle Timothy tapped his earpiece again. "Package is prepped and ready to be picked up. Roger that."

He unzipped another pouch on his vest.

We all flinched. But this time nothing exploded.

UNCLE TIMOTHY'S SPY BOAT DRIFTS AWAY....

HERE WE GO!

ZIP

KA-BLAM

He took his Bluetooth out of his ear and tucked it into the zippered pocket.

"Listen up, Kidds," he said. "Whether you like it or not, you're the only people who can finish what your father started."

"Which was what?" I asked.

"What do you think?"

"Finding Mom! He knew she was alive."

"Whether he knew it or not, Bickford, the Thomas Kidd I know would never abandon hope of retrieving what he considered the most important package on earth, would he?"

"No, sir."

"When we last made contact, he told me he had already plotted his next moves. Sounds like you guys picked up the slack since his disappearance and followed through on phase one."

"Finding the bee amulet?"

"Correct. Your next step will become crystal clear once you study the map he told me about, the one hanging down in The Room."

"The one of the Western Hemisphere?" said Beck.

"Roger that."

"But it's just a pull-down school map."

"Study it again. Look at it differently. Follow the course plotted on the map."

"There was no course!" said Beck, sounding frustrated.

"Your father told me there was," said Dad's CIA boss. "Find it. Don't let that map fall into the wrong hands. I'd say 'good luck,' but you four don't need luck. I've worked with plenty of top-notch agents. I've also seen how you four handle yourselves. Whether you know it or not, you are well on your way to becoming expert operatives. Your parents would be proud."

"Thank you, sir," said Tommy.

"We know karate, too," added Beck.

"I know. Your father showed me your files."

We had *files*? Who knew?

"I have every confidence that you'll get to the bottom of this mess. Just know that your success is critical—for you, your family, your country, and, yes, the world."

Suddenly, I heard a helicopter overhead.

Its thumping rotors became louder and louder.

Uncle Timothy snapped us all a crisp salute. "I'll be watching!" he said, shouting to be heard over the descending whirlybird.

I looked up to see a Black Hawk helicopter hovering above *The Lost.*

Out came a rope ladder. It unfurled and snapped into place directly in front of Uncle Timothy, who hopped on and was hoisted away.

The package was picked up.

I guess that's why Uncle Timothy was so calm about blowing up his boat. He knew he wouldn't need it for the ride home.

CHAPTER 38

"We need to check out that map!" Beck said to Storm the instant Uncle Timothy's helicopter made its Hollywood exit and disappeared behind a bank of towering clouds.

"It's up front," said Storm. "Inside the—"

Fortunately, she did not finish that thought.

Because we were suddenly surrounded by scuba ninjas!

Eight guys in shimmering black wet suits—all of them toting weapons—had scampered up the sides of *The Lost*. They must have been treading water just above the surface (and out of our line of sight), waiting for Uncle Timothy to make his big chopper exit.

Tommy made a mad dash for the deckhouse, hoping to grab the shotgun.

"Chill, dude!" said a diver who'd boarded our stern. His fierce-looking speargun was aimed at Tommy's chest.

Beck, Storm, and I assumed our *hachiji dachi* (ready) karate positions. We were all set to hand-chop and drop-kick the flippers off these frogmen when one of the ninjas raised his dive mask and peeled back his rubber hood to reveal long, greasy hair and a hipster chin beard.

"Yo, karate kids. Chill."

"Uh-oh," muttered Beck at my side. "They're baaaack."

"We come in peace, dudes and dudettes."

It was the same gnarly pirate freak who'd led Beck's kidnap party.

YO. KARATE KIDS. CHILL.

"We don't wanna hurt anybody. The Big Kahuna just needs to see what's behind that steel door."

While the scruffy pirate dude babbled on, I noticed a very fancy crest on the sleeve of his and the other ninjas' dive suits.

"Nathan Collier Treasure Extractors," Storm mumbled.

Nathan Collier. Mom and Dad's number one nemesis. These surfer pirate dudes weren't here to shout "shiver me timbers" or to plunder booty. They were here because Nathan Collier, the worst treasure hunter to ever sail the seven seas (he was so lame he probably thought there were only five), wanted to rip off more of Mom and Dad's brilliant ideas.

"Dad's not here," said Tommy, joining the rest of us in the center of the ninja circle. "He's the only one who ever had a key to that room."

"Uh-oh," said the leader, moving forward, his wet flippers flapping on the deck. "Sounds like the coolaphonic big brother is also a most excellent liar."

"He's telling you the truth," I said. "Dad took the only key with him when he fell overboard."

"Nah, brah," said the leader. "Jadson?" he called to one of his buddies.

"Chyah, Laird?"

"Play that digital dealio for me again."

The pirate named Jadson removed a miniature MP3 recorder from his watertight utility belt.

"You see, little duder," said Laird, "Mr. Collier has all this supercool, totally rad techno gear on his treasure-hunting vessels. He even has this, like...what'd he call it, Jadson?"

"A parabolic microphone."

"Chyah. It's a long-range listening device, so from, like, three hundred yards away, we could poke it up out of our submarine and hear junk like this."

Jadson pressed the Play button.

"Here's the worst part." It was Beck's voice. A

little staticky, but clearly her. *"More than anything, they wanted The Key."*

"Did you tell them where it was?" That was Tommy.

"Um, no." Beck again. *"Only Storm knows where it's hidden, remember?"*

"Oh. Riiiight. Forgot that part, too."

Now we heard Uncle Timothy's voice: *"Well, it seems the pirates shanghaied the wrong daughter. They should've kidnapped Storm."*

Jadson snapped off the MP3 player.

Laird marched up to Storm. "So, Chubba-Wubba, where's the friggin' key?"

CHAPTER 39

Storm looked like she might have a heart attack. Maybe a stroke.

Maybe both at the same time.

So I did what I do best. I started spinning a story.

"Is that all you guys heard?" I asked.

"Chyah," said Jadson, kind of sheepishly. "The parabolic dish is, like, you know, a bowl? So, if you tilt it wrong, a pelican might roost in it and all you'll hear is a big bird slurping down fish—"

"Doesn't matter, little duder," said the tough guy, Laird. "We know your hugantic sister here has the spare key hidden somewhere on board this bucket."

"But you didn't hear us talking about the dive?

Or the kegs of Confederate gold coins, right?"

Laird stroked his chin beard. I had his interest.

"Great, Bick," said Beck, pretending to be annoyed but really trying to help me out. "Why don't you just tell them all about the kegs of Confederate gold—"

"Don't worry, sis," I said. "These guys aren't treasure hunters. They just work for Collier. They don't care that we're sitting right on top of the CSS *Chattahoochee*."

"Gesundheit, bro," said Laird. "At least cover your mouth."

"No, dude," I said. "*CSS* stands for 'Confederate States Ship.' The *Chattahoochee* was a boat. A blockade runner. Captain Stephen Lee 'Cotton Ball' Davis was in command of the swift little steamship. He was making a run out of Savannah, heading down to Cuba to pick up a load of sugar because the Confederate troops loved to suck on rock candy."

"They used to sing that rock candy mountain song all day long," added Beck.

"That's right. And the CSS *Chattahoochee* was carrying ten barrels loaded to the brim with gold coins, enough to pay the Cubanos for all the sugar the Confederacy needed to win the Civil War."

"What happened?" asked the pirate leader, who was leaning in to hear the rest.

"An ironclad Yankee gunboat called the USS *Rattletrap* chased after the *Chattahoochee*. Half the Union Navy, led by Admiral Benbow and Captain Jim Hawkins, joined it out here in the Atlantic. Cannons started blasting. The *Chattahoochee* was

trapped. In a last-ditch effort to outrun the Yankees, Captain Davis ordered those ten heavy kegs rolled over the side of his ship. Without the extra weight, the *Chattahoochee* slipped free and took off for Bermuda."

"Then what?" asked the dude named Jadson.

"The Confederate soldiers never got their rock candy, so the South lost the war. And...no one ever found the dumped gold."

"Until yesterday," said Beck. She pulled out her little pocket sketchbook and whipped up a quick picture of the phony Confederate treasure.

"It's all right down there," I said, gesturing at the ocean just off our bow. "So, come on, Storm. Show these guys The Room. Let them shuffle papers for Nathan Collier. Then the four of us can get back to some *serious* treasure hunting."

"Sounds like a plan," said Beck.

"Hang on," said Laird. "We want the kegs filled with gold coins."

"So you can give them to Nathan Collier?" I asked.

"No, little duder. If there's a mondo mother lode of gold coinage down beneath the swells, then Collier can take my gas. Me and my brohahs will go buy our own submarine!"

Jadson nudged me in the back with his speargun. "Put on your dive gear, little duder. You're taking us down to collect our Confederate gold."

"Fine. But my brother and sister have to come, too."

"Yeah," said Beck. "Bick's not so good with remembering stuff."

"Like where we, you know, found the gold," added Tommy.

"Fine," said Laird. "Gear up. We dive in five."

Tommy, Beck, and I hurried belowdecks to grab our scuba stuff.

"We take 'em under the bow?" said Tommy.

I nodded. "And blast 'em with everything we've got!"

CHAPTER 40

R emember how I told you Dad had custom-
built all sorts of secret cubbyholes and hiding
places into *The Lost*?

Well, since Dad wanted to be prepared for anything, including underwater ambushes, he had the
shipbuilders install an airtight, pressurized com-
partment under the bow of our boat. Stashed inside
were two APS underwater assault rifles.

I used to wonder how Dad got his hands on
a pair of special underwater AK-47s created by
the Soviet Union during the Cold War. Now that

I knew he and Mom were CIA agents, I figured they'd just picked them up on Spy Orientation Day or something.

Underwater, ordinary bullets are seriously inaccurate. They just sort of drift and drop and hit innocent fish. The APS (short for Russian words that mean "Special Underwater Automatic") was designed to fire straight shots when submerged. Plus, it has a longer range and more penetrating power than most spearguns.

In other words, if Tommy and I could get our hands on the two underwater assault rifles stowed in our bow, we might have a chance at fighting off the pirates.

"You sure you guys want to do this?" I said, strapping on my air tanks.

"Definitely," said Tommy. "I'm tired of these gnarly surfer 'dudes' calling me 'dude,' little duder."

"I'm tired of that head goon's ironic facial hair," said Beck.

"We could get, you know, killed."

"Nah," said Tommy. "We're the Wild Things."

"And now," cried Beck, "let the wild rumpus start!"

We headed up to the deck, flippers slapping hard the whole way. We were ready to roar our terrible roars, gnash our terrible teeth, roll our terrible eyes, and show our terrible claws.

"You duders ready to make us all bajillionaires?" sneered the pirate leader.

"You bet," I said, sliding my mask over my eyes and nose.

"What about the fat chick?" I heard one of the pirates say, using his speargun to point at Storm. "Should someone stay on board to guard her?"

"Nah," said Laird. "Shamu the whale is harmless."

I glanced over at Storm.

She had that thundercloud look in her eyes again.

"Let's do this thing!" shouted Laird. He gestured toward the side of the boat. "After you, little duders."

This was good.

They were giving us a head start.

Tommy jumped in first.

"Wait a second," said Beck. "I have a kink in my air hose."

"Hang on, sis," I said, going over to pretend like I was untwisting her line. Then I banged her tank a couple of times like that would fix whatever was wrong. I had to give Tommy as much extra time as possible to pop open our underwater weapons trunk.

"Come on, you two," grumbled the pirate leader. "The surf is awesome. Let's boogie."

"Um, if you don't mind," said Beck, still working on her hose, "I'd like to breathe while I'm underwater."

The pirate pulled out his knife. "We don't really need you down below, dudette."

"Yes, we do," I said as Beck slipped on her mask, popped her regulator into her mouth, and gave us the good-to-go thumbs-up. "Beck found kegs nine and ten. Me and Tommy could only find one through eight."

"Whatever," said Laird.

He shoved Beck off the side of the boat. Then he shoved me.

The two of us sliced into the water, kicked our way clear of our own bubble clouds, and darted like dolphins under the bow of the boat.

Tommy had the cubbyhole open. He saw us and held out his hand, rotating his wrist and pointing up to the weapons cabinet.

It was the diving hand signal for "Something is wrong."

Beck and I swam closer.

The weapons cubbyhole was empty.

My guess? Louie Louie's Cayman crew, the guys who fixed our hull, took home some Russian souvenirs.

There was no time to get angry about it, because that was when I heard the muffled thuds

of eight pirates jumping into the water alongside *The Lost*.

I caught a glimpse of pirate leader Laird's eyeballs, magnified by the glass lens of his diving mask. He looked seriously steamed.

Our only hope was to go hand-to-hand, underwater, against the pirates. There were eight of them, three of us.

And they had spearguns.

A VERY EMPTY WEAPONS HOLD

THiS is NOT GOOD. . . .

CHAPTER 41

One major problem with my plan: You don't do martial arts underwater. When the eight pirates swam after us, we did our best to karate-chop and kick them away. But they had weapons. We had gloved fists and flippered feet.

That's when I realized that somebody might die—*maybe several somebodies.*

But on deck or underwater, we Kidds were still Wild Things.

Tommy yanked the mask off the surfer who had been coming at him with a serrated dive blade. It was the short dude with the ponytail. Freaking out from all the salt water stinging his eyes, he kicked his legs and shot up to the surface.

I saw one of the goons aim his speargun at Beck. I swam over to push her out of the way, but a bad guy grabbed hold of my ankles. I did a backward karate kick and heard the glass in his mask shatter. He let go to clutch his face, and I was free.

I gave Beck a sharp shove. She gave me a dirty "whose side are you on?" look.

Until the barb-tipped spear whooshed between us.

It punctured an air tank strapped to the back
of the pirate trying to rip Tommy's regulator out of
his mouth. That dude—looking like he was riding
a jet pack powered by bubbles—shot up to the surface, too.

Tommy gave me a quick okay hand signal and
an even quicker thumbs-down.

I ducked as another spear whizzed two inches
above my head.

Even though sound can be pretty muffled

underwater, I could have sworn I heard the spear thunk into something behind me.

Was it Beck? Was it my overactive imagination?

I whipped around.

No. It wasn't my imagination. It was Laird, the pirate leader.

He'd been coming up to stab me in the back when the spear went in his arm and out his shoulder. Writhing in pain, he was leaking blood all over the place, and his wound sent up a thick red cloud that drifted through the water like a scarlet jellyfish.

Tommy tapped Beck and me on our shoulders and motioned for us to move away from the bloody pirate, fast.

Blood in the water is never a good thing.

It attracts sharks.

In fact, two of them appeared out of the murky darkness and started circling Laird, who swam into a tight cluster with his remaining "brohahs." None of them were aiming their spearguns or knives at us anymore. They were too focused on the toothy sharks, whose keen sense of smell had just announced that it was dinnertime.

That's when Storm cranked up *The Lost*'s engines and sent our propellers spinning till they were churning up foam like underwater Weedwackers. She must've yanked the throttle into reverse, because the boat suddenly lunged backward, the whirling propeller blades aimed right at the pirate cluster.

(I don't think Storm likes being called Shamu *or* Chubba-Wubba.)

The panicked pirates backed off the stern of our ship, retreating maybe twenty yards so they

could deal with the sharks without being sliced to pieces.

Storm reversed engines, cut the rudder, and positioned the stern of *The Lost* directly over the spot where our air bubbles broke through the surface of the water.

Three nylon ropes with triangular handles plunged into the water.

Tommy motioned to his flippers and peeled them off.

Beck and I did the same.

Then we each grabbed hold of one of the handles anchored to the lines.

Tommy glanced over his shoulder to make sure the sharks still had the pirates penned. Then he jabbed his arm up over his head so it shot through the glimmering surface, giving Storm a solid thumbs-up.

Storm threw the throttle up to full speed ahead. *The Lost* blasted forward like a rocket.

Did I mention that one of our favorite activities is barefoot water skiing? That's right. You can ski without skis if your boat is moving fast enough.

The three of us leaned back on the towline, forced our feet up to the surface, and crunched our abdominal muscles to bring ourselves up and out of the water. In no time, Beck, Tommy, and I were skiing on our bare feet behind *The Lost*. Beck even raised her right hand as if we were doing the water-ski show at LEGOLAND Florida.

It was a blast.

I was sorry the pirates missed it.

But they were too busy being shark bait.

CHAPTER 42

We gave Storm another group hug for being such a genius and saving our bacon, then slipped our stinging feet into soothing sneakers.

But the danger wasn't over.

Before we could even pop open the first bottle of Jamaican Ting soda to celebrate, a widening circle of rippling water appeared off our port side. The ocean churned, swelled, and burbled up bubbles. A periscope appeared and was quickly followed by a gush of tumbling water as a submarine's conning tower lurched up out of the sea.

The letters NCTE were emblazoned on its side.

Five minutes later, Nathan Collier, accompa-
nied by two armed bodyguards, had boarded *The
Lost*.

He was about as short as I am (but always made
sure he was photographed to look taller) and had
a cigar stub jammed between his teeth. He was
wearing his standard "I'm an explorer" costume:
dusty boots (even though we were nowhere near

sand), khaki pants, khaki shirt, and faded leather bomber jacket. As always, his hair was glued into place, with one curl dangling above his left eyebrow. I figured Collier had hair and makeup people on his submarine. Probably a tanning bed, too.

"Good afternoon, Kidds," he said with the sleazy smile he uses on his TV show. (It's on one of the obscure cable networks—the Underwater Weirdo Channel, I think.)

"Collier," said Tommy. (Actually, he kind of spit out the *C* part of *Collier*.)

GOOD AFTERNOON, KIDDS!

Collier slanted an eyebrow. He does that on TV a lot, too. "I see you thwarted my lamebrain shipmates."

"Guess so," I said. "When last we saw them, your pirate pals were auditioning for *Jaws: Part Five*."

"And Parts Six, Seven, and Eight," said Beck.

"A fitting end, I suppose," said Collier with a bored sigh because we weren't talking about him. "My moronic sharks reunited with their own kind. It's so hard to find good thugs these days."

I glanced at his bodyguards.

"Oh, these two aren't insulted by that," said Collier. "They only speak Ukrainian. Now then, children, why aren't you hunting Córdoba's lost galleons? You're supposed be three hundred miles south-southwest of here, trolling for Spanish doubloons."

"You mean that stupid postage-stamp map?" said Storm.

As you can probably tell, she was seething again.

"Yes," said Collier, smacking another puff on his cigar. "You gave up so quickly."

"Because the map was so lame!" I said.

"Of course it was!" snapped Collier. "I drew it so you four would waste time digging up rubbish and stay out of my way!"

"You drew it?" said Beck, narrowing her eyes.

"That's right. When I visited Louie Louie's 'shop' on Grand Cayman, he didn't have the item I sought, so my colleagues and I suggested he do us a small favor—for a handsome fee, of course. He hid that absurdly tiny treasure map in some sort of worthless trinket that he'd then pass on to you children."

Storm reflexively touched the bee pendant, which she'd taken to wearing around her neck on a chain.

"I like Mr. Louie," Collier went on. "He'll do business with anyone willing to do business with him."

"What do you want, Collier?" Tommy said impatiently.

"I want any information you have about your

284

father's quest for the rest of the Pirate King's plunder."

"Er, what?" I said.

"Don't act naive. I know the reason you abandoned your Córdoba dive was to complete your father's mission for the Pirate King, correct?"

"We don't know any pirate kings," I said.

"Is he like a Burger King?" said Tailspin Tommy. "But for seafood instead of burgers?"

"Enough!" shouted Collier. "I want your father's maps and files, and I want them now. Otherwise, you four will end up as something worse than shark bait!"

"Whoa," I said. "Take it easy. What kind of treasure was Dad tracking down for this big-shot-king guy?"

"Artwork."

"Seriously?"

"Come, come, Bickford. Must we continue this silly charade? You know exactly what I'm talking about. A certain rare *objet d'art*?"

"What's that?" said Tommy.

"An art object," said Beck. "Pottery and junk."

"That's right, Rebecca," said Collier. "Artistic artifacts of astronomical value."

"Well," I said, "we don't know anything about art."

"Neither do I," said Collier. "I just know what it's worth to one very serious collector. And now that your dear old dad is out of the picture, there is only one man capable of finding the final treasure on the Pirate King's wish list. Me!"

Collier moved closer to Storm. "I want The Key to the secret room, Stephanie. The room filled with all your father's papers, charts, and files. Where is The Key?"

Storm didn't say a word. Or budge. Or blink. I don't think she was even breathing.

"Have it your way," said Collier. He turned to his bodyguards and shouted a command in Ukrainian.

Immediately, both men raised their weapons and aimed them at Storm's head.

CHAPTER 43

"Whoa!" I shouted. "Wait!"

The bodyguards thumbed back the triggers on their handguns.

"Sorry, Bickford," said Collier. "Ukrainians don't understand the word *whoa*."

"Then stop!"

"You want them to stop?"

"Yes!" Beck yelled.

"Then tell your sister to turn over The Key to The Room. Now!"

Finally, Storm moved. Actually, she sort of slouched into a shrug. "Fine. Whatever. Let's get this over with."

Wow.

I couldn't believe Storm had buckled that quickly.

Then again, I wasn't the one staring down the barrels of two Ukrainian guns.

Storm marched into the deckhouse and down into the galley, where she grabbed a meat cleaver and turned to face us.

Up came the Ukrainian guns again.

"Chill," said Storm. "I need this to retrieve The Key." She picked up a puffy yellow sponge from the sink and whacked it in half. The Key tumbled out with a tinkle. "The Room is in the bow. Follow me."

When we reached The Room, Storm slid The Key into the steel door's dead bolt and gave it a quick flick.

"Go ahead," she said to Collier. "Knock yourself out."

Salivating like a dog that just heard somebody shout "Pork chops!" Collier, trailed by his goons, barged into The Room.

And I realized why Storm had caved so quickly.

All the stuff relating to artwork was gone. Even the corny cartoon about "What's a Grecian urn?" wasn't tucked under the glass blotter anymore. Storm had removed anything and everything from The Room that looked like it was (for whatever reason) important to Dad and Mom.

Collier and his two henchmen yanked open file drawers. They flipped through folders. They even looked inside all the masks and helmets and picture frames still hanging on the walls.

They kept at it for over an hour, checking and rechecking every square inch.

Beck, Tommy, Storm, and I got so bored watching them trash The Room, we went back to the galley to grab a snack. Grilled cheese sandwiches with pickles. We'd lived on the high seas long enough to know that grilled cheese is the best comfort food during a pirate raid.

Finally, Collier and his Ukrainian cronies joined us.

Collier's hair wasn't plastered in place anymore. He had at least three curls dangling over his eyes. And some of his spray-on tan was melting behind his ears. (I don't think he was used to sweating.)

He jabbed a fresh cigar into his mouth.

"No wonder your father jumped overboard," he said with a snide grin. "He was a complete fraud."

"No, he wasn't."

"Oh yes, he was. He had absolutely no information about the final item the Pirate King hired him to locate, even though he'd accepted a very generous retainer when he took on that task. Your father must have known his ineptitude was about to be unmasked, so he took the coward's way out and abandoned his ship—not to mention his children—in the middle of a tropical storm!"

"Get off our boat," said Tommy.

I was right there with him. "Leave. Now."

"Crawl back to your submarine, Collier," added Beck.

"You make me want to vomit," said Storm, "in your face."

None of us cared about the Ukrainians or their weapons anymore.

Nathan Collier had insulted our father.

"Oh, I'll leave," said Collier. "Because someone has to complete the job your father so recklessly abandoned. I always knew he was a terrible treasure hunter." He gestured over his shoulder toward The Room. "Now I have proof."

Collier and his gun ghouls headed out to the deck.

But before he left, Collier turned around to give us one last bit of advice: "And, Kidds? If we ever meet again, I won't be nearly as pleasant as I am right now. In fact, you four will end up dead. I'll make sure of it. Happy sailing!"

CHAPTER 44

R ight after Collier's sleek submarine slipped under the water and disappeared, Storm received yet another group hug for being smart enough to hide all the stuff Dad had hanging on the walls of The Room.

"Way to think ahead," I said.

"Life is like chess," said Storm. "You need to be three moves ahead of your opponent at all times."

"You think Collier will go back and help out those surfer dudes?" said Tommy.

"Maybe," I said. "Maybe not. Should we do it?"

"I say we leave the pirates to Collier or the sharks and go check out that map," said Beck, reminding us what we were about to do before we were boarded by the ninjas in wet suits.

"It's inside the mainmast," said Storm, leading the way toward the prow of the boat.

She tapped the bottom section of the mast, and a wooden panel popped open. Reaching inside the hollow core, she pulled out the rolled-up map. The four of us each took a corner and held it down on the deck.

"Still looks like a school map to me," I said.

"Not to me," said Beck, tilting up her 3-D glasses for a second and then lowering them back to her nose. "This is incredible! It has to be why Mom told me to hang on to these glasses after we saw that 3-D movie together in Cyprus. They're like spy decoder glasses!"

Unbelievable. This was Beck's first time looking at the wall map through her tinted lenses. (Yes, Beck, I was going to remind everybody that the first time you went into The Room, you'd taken off your 3-D glasses because the cabin was so dark.)

"What do you see?" I asked.

"Where we need to head next," said Beck triumphantly.

"New York, right?"

"Nope. Charleston, South Carolina."

"Check it out," said Beck. "George Town on Grand Cayman is circled. And there's some writing: 'Number one: Find bee amulet.'"

"Wait a second," I said. "The same words were on that note Storm found in the file folder."

"Yep," said Beck. "And so was this: 'Number two: Make trade.'"

"We made the trade. With Louie Louie. We gave him the African mask for half of a bumblebee bauble."

"True," said Beck. "But on the map, 'Make trade' is linked to Charleston." She tapped the map on the coast of South Carolina.

"So we need to make another trade," said Storm.

"Yep," said Beck, "and whatever we trade the bee for in Charleston, *that's* what we need to take to Dr. Lewis up in New York so he can authenticate it."

"We have to complete Dad's mission," I said.

"Hello? I've been saying that forever, Mr. Let's Take the Money and Fly to Cyprus."

There was no need for a Twin Tirade. Beck was right.

"Tommy?" I said.

"I'm on it. Laying in a course for Charleston." He jumped up and headed to the wheelhouse. The rest of us rolled up the map and stuffed it back inside the hollow mast.

"Charleston is a big city," said Storm. "Second-largest in the state of South Carolina. Where exactly in Charleston are we supposed to make this trade?"

"Good question," I said. "Let's head back to The Room. Rummage through a few more files."

"Why?" said Storm. "Collier and his Ukrainian knuckle-draggers didn't find anything."

"I know," I said with a sly grin. "But they weren't wearing Beck's supersleuth 3-D glasses."

CHAPTER 45

T he next afternoon, Beck and I were sitting
in folding chairs, sinking into the sand of
Folly Beach, near a spot called the Washout (aka
"Hollywood" and "The Edge of America"), which,

according to Tommy, was where you could catch the best breakers on the whole South Carolina coast. We were under a beach umbrella, combing through another stack of file folders we'd found in The Room. Storm had stayed on *The Lost* to go through the items she'd hidden in case we'd missed something before.

And Tommy? He was riding the waves and hanging with the locals, including this muscle-ripped "surfer chick" named JJ who could stand on one foot at the nose of her board while riding the crest of a curling wave.

"Here we go," said Beck, squinting through her 3-D glasses. "It's about time!"

Beck and I had spent the entire nine-hour journey from our last dive site off the coast of Florida up to Charleston taking turns slipping on the gray shades and reading scholarly junk about archaeology, Egyptology, and all sorts of other *ology*s. Good times. Lots of laughs. (Not.)

"This paper is about excavations on a Spartan hill called Therapne near the River Eurotas, where some scholars think the real Helen of Troy might have had a castle. And get this: It's double-spaced."

She had my interest. Not about Sparta or the real Helen of Troy. The double-spacing. "Can you read something between the lines?"

"Yep. All of it in Dad's handwriting. It says, 'Trade the African Mask for the Minoan bee pendant.'"

"Right. Been there. Done that."

"This is interesting: 'Louie Louie—deals fairly—but with *anyone*.'"

"That's for sure. I still can't believe he helped Nathan Collier."

"I can," said Beck. "Sleazy attracts sleazy. Now write this down: 'Take bee amulet to Portia Macy-Hudson, gray-market art and antiquities, Three Thirty-Three Sunset Lane, Daniel Island, outside Charleston. Make trade for the object.'"

"I'll bet this Portia Macy-Hudson person has the other half of the bee bauble," I said.

"That's my bet, too. After we 'secure the object,' we're supposed to take 'the object' to Dr. Lewis in New York and ask him to authenticate it."

"Um, what, exactly, *is* 'the object'?"

"Dad doesn't say."

"Because he thought he'd be the one making the trade."

Beck nodded. "We just have to hope this Portia person knows what Dad was hunting for."

"The way Louie Louie did."

"Exactly."

Beck closed the file folder.

"You know," I said, "I think I figured out why Dad jotted down his secret notes between the lines of that particular document: Helen of Troy was kidnapped."

"Duh. We learned that when Mom taught us Greek mythology back in second grade."

"But don't you see?" I said enthusiastically. "Dad knew Mom had been kidnapped, too. This mission was—and still is—all about rescuing *her*!"

"That's a stretch," said Beck, rolling her eyes.

"Come on, Beck. Think positive. We're gonna rescue Mom!"

"No, Bick. You need to *grow* up and quit being such a sap."

And right there, on Folly Beach, surrounded by surfer dudes and beach bunnies, Twin Tirade No. 431 erupted like Mount Vesuvius (which we'd recently read about in a file Dad had about the ruins of Pompeii).

"Grow up? I'm two minutes older than you!"

"Then act your age, Bickford. Quit saying we're gonna rescue Mom."

"I will, Rebecca—right after you quit being such a stick-in-the-mud fuddy-duddy."

"Fuddy-duddy? What kind of word is that?"

"It means you're acting like an old fart."

"I am not. I'm just being realistic."

"No, you're being an old poop pessimist."

"Sorry, Bick. But the world is what it is, not what we want it to be."

"It doesn't have to stay that way, Beck."

"You're hopeless."

"No, I'm not."

"Yes, you are."

"I thought you said I needed to quit hoping?"

"Because you do!"

"Well, how can I be hopeless—without hope—if I'm hoping all the time?"

"I don't know."

"Neither do I."

"So there."

"Fine."

We both took a deep breath.

The tirade, like the last wave that just crashed against the beach, was officially done and gone.

Beck spoke first. "You think Tommy's newest girlfriend will give us a ride to Three Thirty-Three Sunset Lane?"

From the way JJ and Tommy were comparing arm muscles and laughing, I had a feeling they might be sending out wedding invitations in a couple of weeks.

"Definitely."

"Cool. Let's boogie."

"And we need to pick up Storm. She's wearing the bee amulet."

"Right." Beck paused. "You know, maybe all of this *will* lead us to Mom, Bick."

I smiled. "Thanks."

"Hey," said Beck, "I want to rescue her, too. I need to thank her for picking the smarter twin to wear these sweet 3-D glasses."

CHAPTER 46

Fortunately, JJ had this amazingly awesome old taco truck that she'd turned into her surfmobile. It was painted bright purple with yellow flower trim and had plenty of room in the back for all of us.

"Your friend must be totally loaded," JJ said as we pulled up in front of the glass-and-stucco mansion on Daniel Island. The place had a five-car garage. Every one of those cars probably had its own private bathroom, too.

"Maybe you should wait out here, JJ," said Tommy.

"Chyah. I'm not really dressed to go museum hopping."

JJ was still in her surfing clothes: a tight shirt that she called a "rash guard," a towel wrapped around her waist, sunglasses, and a bright purple sports watch. And she was right—the big glass building looked like a modern-art museum.

Tommy, Storm, Beck, and I made our way under

a vine-covered arbor into a shady courtyard with a reflecting pool. We climbed a set of white marble steps and knocked on the double doors, made out of bronze hammered to look like a sunset. We rang the bell. A couple of times.

About a minute later, the front doors swung open and a very elegant-looking lady in her early fifties was standing in the foyer. She wore bright red glasses and even brighter red lipstick.

"Yeh-ya-es?" she drawled, staring at us like we were street beggars who'd made a wrong turn somewhere on the mainland. "May I help y'all?"

"Um, are you Ms. Portia Macy-Hudson?"

"Yeh-ya-es?"

(You ever notice how Southern people can make a one-syllable word like *yes* sound like it has three?)

"Wow," Beck blurted out, who was peering around Ms. Macy-Hudson to scan the inside of the house. It had a humongous, sun-filled living room with giant oil paintings hanging all over the two-story-tall white walls. "Is that a Picasso? And that one there, over the fireplace—that's a real Cézanne, isn't it?"

"I'm sorry," said Ms. Macy-Hudson snobbishly, "but who, exactly, are you children?"

"We're Dr. Kidd's kids," I said.

"Who?"

"Professor Thomas Kidd. The world-famous archaeologist and treasure hunter?"

"Oh, yeh-ya-es. Of course. Your father and I conversed over the telephone a week or so ago."

"Mind if we come in?" said Storm, barging into the living room without waiting for an answer. "I sunburn easily."

Ms. Macy-Hudson sputtered in protest as the rest of us trooped in after Storm.

Tommy whistled. "Check it out," he said. "She isn't wearing anything except a flower in her hair and a shoestring around her neck."

"That, young man," sniffed Ms. Macy-Hudson, "is one of Manet's modernist masterpieces. It was inspired, of course, by Titian's *Venus of Urbino*."

"Was Venus naked, too?"

"Of course."

"Man. I definitely need to check out more art museums."

"None of it matches," mumbled Storm, doing a quick scan of the dozen or so paintings. She had, obviously, just called up her photographic memory of the art images pinned to the walls of The Room.

"Do y'all have some reason for bein' here, other than gawking?" Ms. Portia Macy-Hudson asked. "If not, I'll have to kindly ask y'all to—"

She gasped. "Where...did you get that necklace?" Ms. Macy-Hudson asked, pointing to the bee pendant hanging from Storm's neck.

Gasp!

I stepped in to answer. "From a businessman,"
I said coolly. "One who enjoys doing business with
those who enjoy doing business with him."

"Do you enjoy doing business, Portia?" asked
Beck. "Wanna make a trade?"

"For the Minoan bee-goddess pendant?"

"It's a goddess?" said Storm, holding it up inches
from her face.

"You shouldn't be wearing it!" exclaimed Ms. Macy-Hudson. "It's over two thousand years old! The bronze is very, very fragile."

"Chyah!" said Tommy. "It's already, like, busted in half."

"I have the other half!" said Ms. Macy-Hudson, stretching out her arms like a brain-dead zombie. "I need that amulet."

"Fine," I said. "What'll you give us for it?"

"Name your terms!"

"Um, did you and Dad discuss making a deal?"

"Yes!" Her greedy eyes grew wider.

"And what did Dad want in exchange?"

"He wasn't specific. I want the bee. I *need* the bee. I must have the bee!" Realizing she was, basically, going nutzoid on us, she took a second to compose herself. "I will give you anything you desire."

Beck's eyes lit up. "Anything?"

"Anything you see in this house. It's yours. Just name it!"

CHAPTER 47

"D on't y'all see?" said Ms. Portia Macy-Hudson, leading us down a flight of stairs to a lower living room. "I am the reincarnation of the *ancient* Portia, the Minoan mistress known as the Pure Mother Bee, who was chosen by Apollo and gifted with prophecy."

(She was also a wackadoodle, if you ask me.)

The crazy lady's lower living room was even crazier. Every inch was cluttered with bee gewgaws. A fresco of the Sumerian bee goddess. Limestone sculptures of bees. A silk painting of the four-armed Hindi Bhramari Devi, a bee goddess from India who had a swarm buzzing out of her hair. There were even a few framed boxes

Honey Nut
Cheerios

of Honey Nut Cheerios with that cartoon bee.

And, in the center of the bee room, mounted with its own glittering gold chain, was the other half of our bumble-bee bauble.

"When my pen-dant is complete," Portia gushed, her eyes about as wide as honey-baked hams, "I will be the new high priestess of the ancient bee magic! Give me the amulet! Take whatever art you choose!"

"Really?" said Beck. "We can grab that Picasso in the other room? 'Cause it's gotta be worth a bazillion dollars."

"Anything. It's yours. Just give me the bee pendant!"

Okay, this was a little like being handed

a million-dollar gift card in an Apple store—especially for Beck, who *loooooves* art (not that there's anything wrong with that).

"Okay. We'll take the Picasso," she said. "No, wait. The Degas. Or, um, that Cézanne!"

"I want *that* one," said Tommy. (I'm sure you know exactly what painting he was thinking of.)

"That painting back there," said Storm, gesturing at a dark scene of an old-fashioned sailboat being tossed up on a huge wave in a tumultuous storm. "That's Rembrandt's *Storm on the Sea of Galilee*, right?"

MUST... HAVE... NECKLACE...

"My, my. No wonder you are the one wearing the pendant. You have a keen eye for art, my dear."

"No, I don't. That's Beck's department. I just have a photographic memory. That particular Rembrandt was stolen from a Boston museum in March of 1990 along with twelve other pieces of artwork in what is considered the biggest art theft in US history. A case that remains unsolved."

"Is that so?" said Portia, putting on her genteel Southern damsel act. "Why, I had no earthly idea. I am but a middlewoman. I ask no questions."

While she defended herself, a stack of wooden crates padded with dry straw caught my eye. They were stashed inside an open closet.

"What's all this stuff?" I asked.

"New merchandise," said Portia. "Mostly rubbish. It arrived several weeks ago from a Mediterranean acquisitions expert I work with. I haven't had time to catalog or price it."

"Mind if I take a look?" I asked.

"Be my guest."

In one of the crates, I saw a chipped and dirty vase with two jug handles and a footed base. There were scenes painted on the sides in a rusty-clay color against black that reminded me of illustrations in our Greek mythology books. The scene on the side of the vase I could see through the slats showed a young guy chasing after a young girl.

"What's in this crate?" I asked.

"That dirty old thing? A Grecian urn."

"What's a Grecian urn?" asked Tailspin Tommy.

"About thirty dollars a week!" I shouted. "We'll take it!"

CHAPTER 48

I grabbed the wooden crate out of the closet. The instant I did, I swear I could hear Dad's voice in my head saying, *Way to go, Bick. You cracked my corny secret code!*

Unfortunately, in my *ears*, I could hear Ms. Portia Macy-Hudson cackling with glee.

"You could've chosen any of my priceless masterpieces and you chose that? A chipped, old urn? What a foolish, foolish little boy!"

I could also hear Beck. "Are you nuts, Bick? We should take the Rembrandt or the Picasso."

"Or the hottie," said Tommy.

"I'd go with the Rembrandt," said Storm. "I remember the museum's insurance company offered a huge reward for its safe return."

"No!" I said. "This is *the object* we want."

I really tried to lay into those two words hard so Beck would understand that this was why Dad had that corny Grecian urn cartoon under the glass blotter in The Room, why he kept repeating that same lame joke to me all the time. But she didn't get it. I couldn't blame her.

"Let's get out of here," I said. "Fast."

"B-b-but," stammered a totally baffled Beck. "Picasso? Rembrandt?"

"Wait!" shouted the loony queen bee. "I must first take possession of my merchandise and make certain it is the genuine Minoan amulet and not a cheap imitation."

She started flicking her fingers, working her lips, and making weird buzzing noises as she moved toward Storm. She also twitched her shoulders as if she had wings. Yep. She was our very own Honey Nut Weirdio.

"Give her the pendant, Storm," I said.

Storm carefully raised the necklace up over her head and handed the bumblebee to Ms. Portia Macy-Hudson, who received the bauble as if it were the Holy Grail.

"After all these years, it's finally mine!" She was practically panting. She took the amulet and raced over to the dummy neck where the missing twin was on display. "Oh, ancestral bee priestesses of Crete! We are once more complete."

I guessed that meant the two pieces fit.

"I have been searching for this lost relic for years. Decades. Wherever did you find it?"

I was about to answer when a familiar voice broke in. "Why, I know exactly where they found it, Momma!"

And who should sashay into the room but *Daphne*, Tommy's "dumb blond" friend from the Caymans. She wasn't wearing a bikini top and cutoffs today. She was decked out in an all-white tennis outfit with embroidered bees where the polo ponies should've been.

"Hey, Daphne," said Tommy, striking one of his manly poses. "How you doin'?"

UGH.

HOW YOU DOIN'?

This time, the charm wasn't working. Daphne's claws were out. Way out.

"These little brats bartered with Louie Louie, Momma. Gave him an African mask for that bee trinket. I was gonna do the exact same thing, but that one there…"

She pointed her nicely manicured talon at Beck. And judging by the crazed, homicidal look in her eyes, she was an even bigger psychofungalfreak than her mother.

"Why, she came after me with a double-barreled shotgun! And now y'all are gonna see how it feels to be terrorized."

She smashed open a glass case mounted on the wall and pulled out an ancient Aztec sacrificial dagger. It had a beehive handle and a very long, very sharp stinger.

"Run!" I shouted.

This time, no one disagreed with my decision.

The four of us flew out the door, splashed across that reflecting pool, and leaped into the back of JJ's surfmobile.

Daphne, screeching like a banshee, was maybe ten yards behind us.

"We need to boogie," said Tommy.

"Chyah," said JJ, stomping down so hard on the gas pedal I think the taco truck popped a wheelie.

We blasted off. Crazy Daphne chased after us with that bee dagger for about a quarter mile.

When we'd finally lost her, JJ turned to Tommy.

"So, who was that?"

"Just, you know, this flaky chick I met. Down in the islands."

JJ just nodded. "She's a little amped, huh?"

"Totally over the falls."

I looked around inside the back of the truck. No knives, Aztec or otherwise. I figured if JJ ever went all Daphne on Tommy, she'd just bonk him on the head with a surfboard.

CHAPTER 49

As soon as we were back at the marina and safely aboard *The Lost*, Beck and I headed up to the bow pulpit.

I was still carrying the wooden crate holding the Grecian urn. Beck was still mumbling stuff like "We could've had a Picasso or a rare Rembrandt, but *noooo*. Bick wanted the bee queen's old Greek honey jug."

It was definitely time for Twin Tirade No. 432.

"What the heck happened back there, Bickford?"

"I followed the clue!"

"What clue?"

"Dad's corny joke about the Grecian urn."

"He never told it to me."

"Yeah, well, Mom never gave me a pair of 3-D glasses to decode secret messages and maps, either."

"So? Storm knew where The Key to The Room was hidden, and we didn't!" snapped Beck.

"Big deal," I snapped back. "Tommy knew where *the college fund* was hidden!"

"So what?" screamed Beck. "You think Mom and Dad gave us each some kind of special clue that they didn't give to anybody else?"

"Yes, now that you mention it, I do think that!" I screamed back.

"Well, I thought it first."

"I know you did."

"That's why I said it before you did."

"I know."

"Okay."

"Good."

"We're cool?"

"Totally."

We both took a breath.

"What's that?" said Beck, pointing to something on the side of the urn's crate I couldn't see. I flipped the wooden box around.

There was a stencil spray-painted on one of the wooden slats: a copper-colored silhouette that kind of looked like a very pudgy, one-legged rhinoceros. Or a pork chop someone had been chomping into. Beneath the copper inkblot were two crossed olive branches.

HMMM...

Fortunately, while Beck and I were staring at the strange marking, Storm wandered up to the bow. "Interesting," she said, studying the stencil mark. "Guess that Grecian urn was originally supposed to go to Cyprus before someone stole it and shipped it off to *Aunt Bee's Antiques Theft Show*."

The instant Storm said that, Beck and I took over.

"Of course," said Beck. "It's the silhouette of the island of Cyprus."

"The silhouette is copper," I said, remembering Mom's homeschool World Flags lecture, "because the name *Cyprus* comes from the Greek word for 'copper.'"

"What's going on, you guys?" said Tommy, who had just said buh-bye to JJ in the marina parking lot.

"Bick is a genius!" said Beck.

"Nah, that's Storm's department."

"True," said Storm with a shrug. "No brag. Just fact."

"This has to be the object Dad wanted us to swap for," Beck continued.

"It was supposed to be shipped to Cyprus," I chimed in. "Where those thugs have Mom."

"This could be the key to getting her back," said Beck.

I tipped the crate so I could look between the slats nailed to the top of the box and peered down into the mouth of the jug.

"Guys! There's something stuffed inside the urn! It looks like an envelope."

"Bring the box back to the stern," said Tommy. "I'll grab a pry bar."

Beck and I carefully toted the crate to the rear of the boat. Tommy came up from the hull cabins with a crowbar.

"Don't shatter the urn," said Storm.

Tommy pried off the four wooden slats on the top of the crate. Once that was done, Storm used our hot dog tongs to remove the envelope from inside the ancient piece of pottery.

I was immediately confused.

ZOOM SOSIBIOS VASE PROVENANCE PAPERS

"What are provenance papers?" I asked.

"Documents that help you prove a valuable piece of art isn't a fake," said Beck.

"So this urn is valuable?" I said.

"There's only one way to find out for sure," said Beck. "Get an expert to authenticate it."

"Dr. L. Lewis," said Storm. "Professor of Ancient

Near Eastern Art and Archaeology, Eighth Floor, Schermerhorn Hall, Columbia University, New York, New York, 10027."

"On it," said Tommy. He climbed up to the wheelhouse and plotted our new coordinates.

Ten minutes later, *The Lost* was back out on the ocean, sailing north to New York City.

It was time to meet Dr. Lewis.

PART 3

IN THE
PALACE
OF THE
PIRATE KING

CHAPTER 50

When we slipped into New York Harbor and made our way past the Statue of Liberty, there were so many boats—barges, cruise ships, pleasure craft, sailboats—any one of them could've been following us.

Or we might've just been paranoid.

Learning that both of your parents work for the CIA will do that to you.

We sailed up the Hudson River and docked at the West 79th Street Boat Basin, not too far from Dr. Lewis's office on the Columbia campus near

WE ARRIVED DURING **RUSH HOUR**.

West 118th Street. When we tied off at the pier, the wheelhouse computer bonged with an e-mail alert.

It was from Uncle Timothy:

> **Chatter in Charleston suggests you have moved closer to achieving your objective. Congratulations. I have arranged, through friends, for you four to spend the night at the Plaza Hotel.**

The Plaza Hotel is the fanciest hotel in all of New York City.

It's also where Mom and Dad spent their honeymoon and where we all stayed a couple of times back when we were one big, happy family.

So Tommy wrapped the Grecian urn in a soft (and stinky) sweatshirt and stuffed it into a gym bag. We hailed a taxi and headed across town to check into the luxurious hotel.

"Time for our horse ride!" said Beck.

"Definitely," said Tommy.

Carriage drivers always wait just outside the

hotel, a kind of castle near the southern edge of Central Park. In fact, Dad always joked that the Plaza costs more than most hotels because "it has more horsepower."

Yeah. Dad liked a good corny pun.

As we clip-clopped up a winding hill in Central Park, we were all totally silent for a long, long time.

I was thinking about Dad and Mom and the

last time we took this same carriage ride. I guess everybody else was, too.

"I'd rather be sitting on Dad's lap," said Beck.

"With Mom naming all the statues and junk," added Tommy.

"And then, at night," whispered Storm, "they'd sit with me on the hotel room floor and help me memorize the subway map."

"Hey," I said, trying to change the subject before everybody (including the carriage driver and his horse) started sobbing. "After the carriage ride, let's go grab something to eat."

"Serendipity!" everyone shouted at the same time, including me. Serendipity 3 was Mom and Dad's favorite restaurant in New York, probably because they served this awesome dessert called "Frrrozen Hot Chocolate."

There were all sorts of family memories packed inside the famous restaurant's wildly decorated walls. So even though we were sipping the happiest ice-cream-and-chocolate concoction ever created, we were all feeling sort of sad.

But halfway through dessert, Beck leaned over and whispered something in my ear: "Don't worry. The next time we're here, there'll be two more straws in the whipped cream. One for Mom."

I finished her thought: "And one for Dad."

CHAPTER 51

E arly the next morning, after a swanky Plaza Hotel breakfast of bacon, eggs, and toast that cost thirty-three dollars (per person), we headed off to Columbia University with the Grecian urn packed inside Tommy's bulky gym bag.

But the instant we stepped out of the grand hotel's even grander doors and walked down the extremely grand red-carpeted steps to the sidewalk, I felt like we were being watched.

"You guys?" I said, nudging my head at three young dudes in sunglasses, board shorts, and Hawaiian shirts—the baggy kind that hide shoulder holsters. All three of them had curly-pigtail

NOTE TO SURFER THUGS:
NEXT TIME, TRY TO BLEND IN A LITTLE BETTER, GUYS.
SERIOUSLY. MANHATTAN BEACH is in L.A., **NOT** MANHATTAN.

wires coming out of earpieces, making them look like Secret Service agents on a tropical vacation. All three were focused on the four of us.

"Stay cool," said Tommy, who was toting the gym bag. "We need to lose these hiddie dodes."

(I had no idea what my big brother had just said. JJ the surfer chick had taught Tommy a ton of surfer slang during their brief time together.)

344

To avoid the "hiddie dodes," we strolled around a grand and gurgling water fountain and headed over to Fifth Avenue.

The three New York City surfers headed that way after us.

"Come on," Tommy said when we hit East Fifty-Seventh Street. He led us down the block to the arched glass front of Niketown. Not because he needed a new pair of kicks. Because he knew the place would be jam-packed crowded.

We darted into what was basically the New York City Sneakers Museum. All sorts of mannequins were decked out in cool Nike gear. The walls were splashed with shoes in more colors than the inside of a jumbo bag of M&M's. Throbbing music blasted through the five-story-tall atrium.

"We need to lose those three," I said. "I think they're *surfers.*"

"Nothing wrong with surfers," said Tommy. "JJ was cool."

"Yeah," said Beck. "But the three tailing us look like trouble."

"We could take the escalators to the fifth floor

and duck out the fire exit to take the steps back down to the street," said Storm, who had already memorized the store's fire-evacuation floor plans.

"Let's 'Just Do It,'" said Tommy, quoting the Nike slogan plastered everywhere.

Storm got on the escalator first, with Beck and me right behind her. Tommy brought up the rear—after he spent a couple of seconds checking out some gnarly water shoes.

Riding up the escalator between the second and third floors, I saw a short guy in a "Hang Twenty" T-shirt heading down on the other side. He had his hair pulled back in a ponytail. A very familiar ponytail.

I looked at Beck. She looked at me.

"Move it, you two," whispered Tommy, coming up behind us. "We need to lose ponytail."

I agreed. The little dude might want us to buy him a new scuba tank to replace the one we'd speargunned back in the shark-infested waters.

We started taking the escalator steps two at a time. Until we bumped into Storm. She wasn't budging.

"What's your problem, Bick?" she asked.

"Pirates," I said through clenched teeth. "The ones we left for the sharks to clean up."

"Impossible. Do you know the odds of surviving a shark attack?"

I never got to hear the answer.

Because when we reached the third floor, we saw another familiar face. This one had a tiny triangle beard on its chin. Laird, the pirate leader. His arm was in a sling, and from the way he glowered at us, I was guessing he could still feel the sting of the salt water in the shoulder wound we gave him.

CHAPTER 52

L aird touched his left ear with his right hand (because his left arm was the one in the sling).

He had an earpiece like the three guys in the sunglasses and Hawaiian shirts, who, when I looked behind us, had just reached the second floor and were talking into their shirtsleeves.

"Welcome to New York City, little duders," said Laird. "Home of Wall Street brokers and other assorted land sharks. Mr. Collier needs to have a word with you four."

"Okay," I said, "here's the word: run!"

The four of us tore through the store like wild things.

"Out of our way, people!" Storm shouted. "Move it or lose it! Coming through!"

Laird came limping after us. I figured one of those sharks had chomped on his leg (or nibbled on his toes) before he and his pirate pals had somehow escaped.

"Whoa!" said Tommy, bringing up the rear. "Check out those shoes!"

Figures. We might be running for our lives, but that didn't mean Tommy couldn't admire the cool merchandise displayed all around us.

"Hey," shouted one of the Nike workers as we raced past a whole row of soccer mannequins. "You can't run in here!"

"Of course we can!" I shouted back. "In fact, that's what we're doing right now."

"We want to make sure our new running shoes work," added Beck. "So far, so good!"

Storm led us to the elevators and jabbed the Down button.

The doors whooshed open.

We hopped in.

The doors whooshed shut.

Just as Laird and his three surfer buds lunged into view.

"They'll take the stairs," I said. "Or the escalators. Either way, we'll beat them to the lobby."

"Then what?" said Storm. "More running?"

"Definitely," said Tommy. "You up for it, sis?"

"Totally."

The doors slid open, and we flew toward the exit.

"Hey, no running!" shouted another Nike person.

"Sorry!" I shouted back. "We couldn't find any walking shoes."

We slammed out the front doors.

"Taxi!" shouted Storm.

Unbelievably, there was one parked right at the curb.

"This is our lucky day!" said Beck.

Except, in the nanosecond it took for her to say that, a businessman in a trench coat grabbed the door handle and stole our cab!

"West," said Storm. "We need to head over to Broadway and hop on the subway up to Columbia."

We were about to take off when I heard skateboard wheels rumbling over concrete behind us.

I turned around and saw another twentysomething guy in sloppy clothes surfing up the sidewalk on a skateboard. The guy was gunning straight at us.

It was Jadson, Laird's second-in-command.

CHAPTER 53

At this point, I'd like to apologize to the hot dog vendor whose cart we knocked over as we raced down Fifth Avenue past Trump Tower: Sorry about that, sir. But if the five-second rule applies on the streets of New York, I hope you were able to grab all those wieners out of the gutter and sell them to folks who like crunchy stuff for lunch.

Fortunately, Jadson wiped out when the hot dog wagon's umbrella toppled over and tripped him up.

When we hit East Fifty-Third Street, we ran

across Fifth Avenue and were, suddenly, on West Fifty-Third Street.

"That's just how they drew the map, Bick," said Storm, when she saw the look of confusion on my face. "Deal with it."

Unfortunately, on the steps of Saint Thomas Church, on the north side of the street, I saw three more surfer-guys, in blousy Hawaiian shirts and Ray-Bans, working their cell phones.

They'd seen us, too.

"Man," I said. "I'm *really* starting to hate surfers."

"This way," said Beck. "The Museum of Modern Art is right up this block."

"And that's helpful, how?" I asked.

"Hey, if we're gonna die, we might as well do it in front of Van Gogh's *Starry Night* or Monet's *Water Lilies*."

We hurried up the crowded sidewalk, hurdling over this unbelievable chalk masterpiece a guy had spent all morning drawing on the concrete.

The three surfer goons were right behind us.

The Museum of Modern Art

Looking over my shoulder, I could see their blond heads bobbing up and down above the mob of sidewalk art lovers as the surfer dudes tried to keep tabs on where we were headed.

We pushed through the MoMA's big glass doors. (*MoMA* means "Museum of Modern Art," not "mother," by the way. Beck also tells me it's pronounced *moh-mah*, not *momma*. I just told her I don't really need to pronounce stuff to write it down. She just suggested I get a life.)

There were about a million people waiting in a long line snaking through the museum lobby and back out to the sidewalk.

A guard in gray slacks and a blue blazer came up to us.

"Yo, kids. The line starts outside. Unless you're members. Then youse can check in at the membership desk."

I hesitated. "Well, um—"

The three surfer dudes slammed through the glass doors.

I stopped hesitating. "We'd like to buy a family membership!"

The guard jabbed his thumb over his shoulder. "See the lady at the desk." He moved away to deal with the three new intruders. "Yo. Hawaii Five-O. This is a museum here. There's no running in museums."

While the guard kept the surfers busy, I handed the membership lady five one-hundred-dollar bills.

"Will that cover us?"

"Are you four a family?"

"Yes, ma'am."

"A family membership is $175."

"Then give us a few of them. We're in a hurry."

We cut across the sculpture garden, dashed down a couple of halls lined with weird paint splotches and portraits of soup cans, and headed out an exit on the far side of the building.

For good measure, we ran across the street, raced around the corner, and headed over to the Hilton Hotel, where there was a long line of yellow taxicabs.

"May I help you, children?" asked a uniformed doorman.

"Yes, sir," I said, pulling another one-hundred-dollar bill out of my pocket. "Our father said you might be able to help us find a taxi if I gave you a tip."

The doorman immediately blew his whistle, and a cab screeched up the covered driveway.

The driver behind the wheel looked like a maniac. (I'm told that most taxi drivers in New York are maniacs.)

"Um, Bick?" said Beck when she saw the bug-eyed loon. "Maybe we should just walk to Columbia."

"No," said Storm, crawling into the cab. "I'm tired of running *and* walking."

Beck and I slid into the backseat with Storm. Tommy sat up front with the driver. Before he had even closed the door, we were zooming away

from the hotel, horn blaring, our driver squeez-
ing his cab between lanes and mumbling under
his breath. We skated through yellow lights, flew
around Columbus Circle, and were off like a shot
up Broadway toward Columbia.

No way were those surfer dudes going to catch
up to *this* wild ride!

CHAPTER 54

We made it up to Columbia University. Alive.

"There's Schermerhorn Hall," said Beck, pointing to a redbrick building with a roof the same green as the Statue of Liberty.

"It was built in 1896," said Storm. I guess she had memorized a college brochure. "The inscription over the doorway says 'Speak to the earth and it shall teach thee.'"

"Really?" said Tommy. "College kids talk to dirt?"

"Come on," I said. "We need to find the Department of Ancient Near Eastern Art and Archaeology."

We entered the building and took an elevator up to the eighth floor. Tommy was still lugging the Grecian urn in his gigantic gym bag.

When we stepped into the hallway, we heard a student say, "Thank you, Professor Lewis!"

"You are most welcome, Kathryn. Most welcome, indeed."

His voice sounded sort of familiar. Kind of wet and slobbery around the vowels.

Beck rapped her knuckles on his office door.

"Professor Lewis?"

"Come in, come in."

The four of us stepped into a little office crammed with books and papers stacked to the

360

ceiling. It was also crammed with Dr. Lewis, who probably weighed three hundred and fifty pounds and looked like he might burst through the arms of his creaky wooden chair. He had chubby cheeks and slicked-down curly hair parted in the middle. He wore a rumpled tweed sport coat, a wrinkled button-down shirt, a hula girl necktie, and blue jeans.

"Are you four in my lecture series?" he asked, peering over the top of his glasses.

"No," I said. "We're Dr. Kidd's children."

"Indeed? Ah, yes. My brother suggested that you might be coming to see me."

"Your brother?"

"My *twin* brother. A very interesting, shall we say, 'antiquities dealer' down in the Cayman Islands."

Beck shot me a look. *Was it possible?*

"Are you talking about Louie Louie?" I said.

"Indeed. He spells his last name differently than I, but for that eccentricity we must blame our parents, who thought twins should share everything, including both their names. To appease the officials at the birth registry, however, they spelled our two names slightly differently. He is Louis with an *ou*, and I am Lewis with an *ew*."

"Wow," said Beck. "Now that you mention it, you do sort of look like Louie Louie."

(That was *very* PC of Beck. Because she could've said, "Wow. You both look like blimps who escaped from the Macy's Thanksgiving Day Parade.")

"The fact that Louis and I are twins," the professor continued, "is why you children ended up with the bee amulet. My brother tells me he was sorely tempted to renege on his deal with your father and sell the Minoan bauble to Nathan Collier. But he gave your father his word. And he has a soft spot for twins."

"Don't we all?" said Storm (somewhat sarcastically, if you ask me).

"Now, then," said Professor Lewis, "how may I be of assistance?"

"Well, sir," I said, "as you may know, our mom sort of disappeared—"

Dr. Lewis clucked his tongue. "Oh, yes. Pity she got caught up in this mess. One of the finest archaeological minds I have ever known. An expert's expert at authenticating ancient artifacts."

"That's why we need you," said Beck.

Tommy hoisted the gym bag up onto the professor's desk.

"Oh, my. What's in the bag?"

"An object we picked up in Charleston, South Carolina," I explained.

"From Ms. Portia Macy-Hudson?"

"Yeah," said Beck. "The wackaloon with bees in her brain."

"Indeed?" Professor Lewis rubbed his chubby hands together, raccoon-style. "Might I examine your treasure?"

"Please do," I said. "We're hoping, since Mom's not around, you can authenticate it for us."

"I will do my best, children." He carefully unzipped the gym bag.

"It's inside my wadded-up sweatshirt," said Tommy. "Sorry about the BO."

The professor carefully unwrapped the bundle.

"Oh my!" He gasped. "Could it be?"

He extracted the provenance papers from inside the antique jug and read what was written on them. Then he gasped again. "Oh, my!"

"What is it?" I asked.

"The Grecian urn."

"Um, we knew that," said Beck.

"I'm sorry. I should be more precise. It is the Attic shape overwrought with marble men and maidens."

"Huh?" He'd totally lost me.

"Children, this is *the* Grecian urn. The very one the great English poet John Keats wrote about in 1819. Surely you are familiar with his 'Ode on a Grecian Urn'?"

"The final lines," said Storm, "declare that 'beauty is truth, truth beauty—that is all ye know on earth, and all ye need to know.'"

"Matey," I mumbled, because that was what Dad had scrawled in the margins of his Grecian urn cartoon in The Room—*"That is all ye need to know, matey."*

His scribble had been another clue!

"This priceless treasure," said Professor Lewis, staring at the clay pot in awe, "this humble but beautiful urn is the very reason your mother is missing."

"What?" we all yelled together.

"It will also, I am quite certain, set her free!"

CHAPTER 55

"Mom's alive?"

"Are you sure?"

"How, exactly, do we save her?"

"So, like, how's this Greek water jug gonna set her free, doc?"

Yes, we more or less bombarded Dr. Lewis with questions. He did his best to quickly explain.

"Several months ago," he said, "multibillionaire art collector Athos Aramis—a notorious international arms dealer known as the Pirate King because he has outfitted so many ne'er-do-wells and scallywags with weaponry—was about to complete a top secret antiquities-for-arms deal in Cyprus."

"Cyprus is where the thugs kidnapped Mom!" I said.

"Indeed. Mr. Aramis—who, by the by, lives here in New York City—sent your mother, whom he trusted and often used in transactions of this sort, to analyze the art and antiquities the Cypriot scoundrels were using to pay him for their weaponry. When it came time to authenticate the Grecian urn, which the Cypriots claimed was the very Sosibios vase that the poet Keats had drawn upon as the inspiration for his famous ode, your mother declared the urn to be a fake."

"Why?" I asked. "I thought you said this was the one!"

"It most certainly is. But *this* urn was stolen off a cargo vessel bound for Cyprus by another band of marauding pirates and eventually found its way to Ms. Portia Macy-Hudson down in South Carolina. The urn the Cypriots were paying Mr. Aramis with was a fake, as your mother declared. Your father and I had been diligently tracking the true urn's whereabouts and finally learned that it was on its way to Charleston."

"So these creeps in Cyprus," said Beck. "They kidnapped Mom because she told the truth?"

"Oh, yes. You see, the truth squelched their deal with the Pirate King. Once your mother declared the urn to be a counterfeit, Mr. Aramis refused to give those Cypriot rascals their weapons. The Cypriots, in turn, swore they would not release your mother, Mr. Aramis's personal envoy, until they received all the weapons they had been promised in the art-for-arms swap. As you might imagine, negotiations between the two parties have been at something of a standstill because neither side is in possession of the authentic Keats urn."

"But now we have it," I said.

"Indeed," said Dr. Lewis.

"This was Dad's mission," said Beck. "To find the real urn and then use it to rescue Mom."

I nodded. "And now it's up to us to finish the job for him!"

CHAPTER 56

T alk about being stunned.

Mom, whom we'd just learned was a CIA agent, was also acting as a go-between for a notorious arms dealer known as the Pirate King? Meanwhile, she was also helping Dad run the treasure-hunting business, homeschooling the four of us, and making the best fish tacos on the planet.

Our mother was one serious multitasker.

"Wait a second," Beck said to Professor Lewis. "Dad had all sorts of photographs of French paintings plastered on the walls of his, er, office. What's up with those?"

"I imagine most of those would be the paintings your father had personally procured for Mr. Aramis on an earlier job. The rest were the artworks to be provided by the Cypriot bandits in exchange for the weaponry. In fact, your father helped Mr. Aramis put together the list of, shall we say, 'missing' artworks he wanted the terrorists to bring to the deal."

I almost gave myself whiplash when I heard that. "Terrorists?"

"Well," said Professor Lewis, "I use the term loosely. Let's just say the gentlemen in Cyprus are not very nice. Thieves and smugglers and riffraff."

"But Mr. Aramis is a bad guy, too, right?"

"Oh, yes. Indeed. In fact, I would daresay that Athos Aramis is one of the worst bad guys currently residing on the FBI's most-wanted list. He's sold weapons to many of America's mortal enemies. He's ruthless, extremely violent, and liable to lash out if backed into a corner. I've also heard that he's extremely cruel to children and small animals."

"And Mom and Dad work for this guy?" I was aghast. Astonished. Horrified. All of the above. "Mom authenticates his Grecian urns and Dad hunts down art treasures for him?"

"Indeed, but this art-for-arms deal was just one small part of a much bigger operation involving Aramis and his shady dealings."

"You're lying," said Tailspin Tommy. "No way would Mom and Dad work for a skeevoid like Aramis. Storm? You got any more of that truth juice?"

"Back on the boat."

"Good. We need to give this troll a shot in the butt and make him stop lying about Mom and Dad."

"I am not lying, children. But—"

"No," I said. "Don't you dare tell us that Mom and Dad were frauds. That they were only pretending to work for the CIA so they could make a ton of money working for this Aramis creep instead."

"Fine," said Professor Lewis with a mysterious twinkle in his eye. "I won't tell you that. Because in your hearts, you already know the real truth."

CHAPTER 57

B efore we left his office, Professor Lewis insisted that we take one of his business cards.

"Call me anytime. Day or night. If I can be of assistance in any way—"

"You've done enough," said Tommy, who was giving the professor the stink eye as he repacked the Grecian urn inside his grimy sweatshirt so he could stuff it back into the gym bag.

Beck grabbed the provenance papers and jammed them inside her back pocket. "Let's get out of here."

"I assure you, children, I meant no disrespect. Your parents were my close, personal friends. I urge you to step back and look at the bigger picture—"

"No, thanks," I said. "We're done looking at pictures. Especially ones you say Dad stole for a cutthroat criminal creep."

The four of us trooped out of the office and stomped down the stairs. We were too steamed to wait for the elevator. We came out of Schermerhorn Hall and hiked across the college campus. Nobody said a word.

"We should go back to the boat," I finally suggested. "We need to figure out how to get in contact with this Athos Aramis. Maybe if we give him the real urn, he can persuade the bad guys in Cyprus to let Mom go."

"He's in Dad's address book on the computer," said Storm, no doubt summoning up the *A* listings in her photographic memory.

"Cool. We'll take the—"

Suddenly, a Frisbee bopped Tommy in the head.

"Whoops! Sorry!" said these four giggling college girls who came scampering over to retrieve their flying disc.

"Are you hurt?" cooed the blond.

"Nah," said Tommy, letting the girls check out his grin and dimples. He rapped his forehead with his knuckles. "I'm thick as a brick up here."

More giggles.

"Let me take a look," said the short redhead. "I'm pre-med."

"Really?" said Tommy, using his cheesiest suave-dude voice. "Maybe we could study some anatomy together."

The rest of us rolled our eyes. This is how Tommy deals with stress and bad news: He flirts with girls.

"Give me a boost so I can check out the injury site," said the short doctor-to-be.

"Cool," said Tommy. "I'll do anything to help advance medical science." He set his gym bag down on the ground so he could grab the giggly redhead with both hands and hoist her up.

But the redhead never gave him that chance.

Instead, she kicked him—right where every doctor in the world knows it will hurt a guy the worst.

Tommy buckled in agony.

The second blond grabbed the gym bag and started running. Fast.

I made a move to chase after her, but the brunette flashed a nasty-looking knife in my face.

"Back off, butt crumb, or you're doggie meat!"

"Surfer chicks," groaned Tommy, still doubled over in pain. "They're surfer chicks."

"Chyah," said the redhead. "Stay off our concrete beach, hotdoggers, or Nathan Collier will go
totally kamikaze on you dudes. You four need to
leave New York. Leave today!"

Then she ran off after the rest of her friends.

Meanwhile, the girl with the gym bag had made
it all the way over to Broadway, where she hopped
into a waiting convertible and sped off. The guy
behind the wheel was short and had a ponytail.

"Collier's pirates took the urn," said Storm,

stating the painfully obvious. "We can't use it to rescue Mom."

The four of us stood there staring blankly as the three other surfer chicks disappeared into the crowds of college kids changing classes.

We were devastated.

No, we were destroyed.

We were also probably the dumbest kids to ever set foot on the Columbia University campus.

CHAPTER 58

O f all the horrible stuff to happen to us since Mom disappeared, this was probably the worst.

Because we'd lost the key to getting her back.

The Grecian urn was gone. So were our dreams of being reunited with our mother on the sunny beaches of Cyprus. Overwhelmed by exhaustion and serious sadness, we headed back to the West Seventy-Ninth Street Boat Basin and *The Lost*.

"It's all my fault," moped Tommy. "First Daphne. Then Miss Pre-Med. Girls are nothing but trouble. I may never flirt again."

While Tommy went up to the wheelhouse

to sulk and Storm hit the galley to find some Ben & Jerry's that we could drown our sorrows in, Beck and I started cranking on Dad's computer down in The Room. We wanted to dig up everything we could find on Mr. Athos Aramis because we both knew that was where Nathan Collier would soon be peddling his stolen goods. If we could be there when the deal went down, maybe we'd still have a shot at rescuing Mom.

Most of the intel on Aramis was pretty ugly stuff. It seemed as if the government had been chasing the slick and extremely well-connected weasel for years, but they could never prove he had done anything illegal.

"He lives at Nine Eighty-Three Fifth Avenue,

right off Central Park," Beck reported. "Extremely swanky address. And, of course, he owns the penthouse apartment."

"What's the security situation?"

"Tight."

"We need to go after Aramis," Storm announced, coming into The Room.

"Um, that's what we're working on," said Beck.

"Good," said Tommy. He'd followed Storm in. "We have to get the urn back—no matter what."

"Don't worry, you guys," I said. "We will. Of course, we have to figure that an international arms dealer like Mr. Aramis is going to have some major firepower at his disposal."

"Major muscle, too," added Beck.

Storm nodded grimly. "His heavily armed security guards will most likely blast us with a Stinger missile. Maybe a rocket-propelled grenade. We'll be dead before we reach the second floor."

"Maybe not," said Beck. "Because the Grecian urn isn't much good to Mr. Aramis without these." She pulled out the provenance papers she had stuffed into her back pocket not long before the surfer chicks stole Tommy's gym bag.

"You grabbed those?" said Tommy.

"Yep."

"Beck, you're the best. You have single-handedly restored my faith in womankind."

"We're gonna need you, too, Tommy," I said.

"No problemo. What do you want me to do?"

"Kick some big-time butt," said Beck.

"Cool. I can handle that. Whose butt am I going for?"

"Mr. Athos Aramis himself," I said. "Beck and I think we should pay him a visit. Tomorrow. High noon."

"Awesome. Come on, Storm. Let's head up to the deck. I need to practice a few of my butt-kicking karate moves."

While Tommy and Storm were off practicing their karate, Beck and I worked on our plan of attack. Okay, maybe it was more of a plan for a suicide mission. But we had to do something.

A little after midnight, I called Professor Lewis.

"Thank you for giving us your number, sir," I said.

"My pleasure, Bickford."

"I hope we're not calling too late."

"Oh. no. Anytime. Day or night."

Beck leaned in so she could hear both sides of the conversation.

"Sorry we got so emotional in your office," I said.

"No need to apologize," replied Dr. Lewis. "This is a very emotional situation."

"Well, anyway, we decided to step back and try to see the big picture."

"Ah, yes. The forest instead of the trees. The ocean instead of the waves. The room instead of the sofa. The—"

"Right," I said, cutting him off. "Here's the deal: We're going over to Fifth Avenue tomorrow to visit Mr. Athos Aramis."

"Oh-ho. You're joking. Right?"

"Nope. Tomorrow. Noon. We're dropping by his Fifth Avenue penthouse."

"Oh, my. I cannot allow this. Mr. Aramis is a very dangerous man. *Lethally* dangerous. What part of 'weapons dealer' don't you understand? You children could end up dead!"

"We know the risks involved. However, Dr. Lewis, in our parents' absence, *you* are not our legal guardian. Uncle Timothy is. Timothy Quinn. Do you know him?"

"Yes." Dr. Lewis's voice squeaked a little.

"Well, if you have issues with what we're about to do, I suggest you give Mr. Quinn a call. Do you have his number?"

"Of course."

"Good. Tell him to hurry. Like I said, we're going in at noon tomorrow."

Beck and I spent the rest of the night down in The Room trying to dig up more info online about Mr. Aramis. He was cunning. Clever. Had an IQ of 202—so he would've been in the *Guinness Book of World Records* if he weren't so "publicity shy." He was also a "noted philanthropist" in New York City. That meant he wore a tuxedo to a lot of fancy charity balls and donated a ton of money to buy the respect—and probably the protection—of the city's most powerful people. He also spent, like, forty thousand dollars on his suits. For each one.

To make things even worse, Athos Aramis absolutely despised children. Thought they were too loud and noisy. In fact, he liked to quote the comedian Henny Youngman on the subject: "What is a home without children? Quiet!"

After a few more hours studying Mr. Aramis and Google maps of his block on Fifth Avenue, Beck and I both fell asleep in front of the computer.

I vaguely remember Tommy coming into The Room and carrying me to my bed.

I think I said "Good night, Dad" when he tucked me in.

"Good night, Bickford," Tommy said back. He even tried to make his voice sound deeper like Dad's when he said it.

Yeah. It was kind of sweet.

Every so often, Tailspin Tommy is like that.

CHAPTER 59

The next morning, over Pop-Tarts, Beck and I launched into Twin Tirade No. 433.

Storm and Tommy ignored us and stayed quietly focused on their frosted rectangular toaster pastries.

"I've been thinking," said Beck. "Visiting Aramis is too risky."

"No risk, no reward," I snapped back in reply.

"Well, what's the reward if we end up dead?"

"Setting Mom free."

"And how will we even know she's free if we're dead?"

"That's not the point, Rebecca."

"Uh, yes, it is, nubby boy."

"Huh?"

"You're a nub. You know—a thing that's point-less. You're nubby."

(My sister, the wordsmith.)

"Look," I said, "sometimes you just have to go with your gut. Like I did when I grabbed the Grecian urn instead of a Picasso."

"You mean the last time we all came *this close* to getting killed."

"Hey, close only counts in horseshoes."

"And hand grenades."

"And bad breath."

"Stick with the hand grenades, Bick."

"Why?"

"Because Mr. Aramis is an *arms dealer*, remember? That means he could have all sorts of weapons, including hand grenades and rocket launchers to shoot them with."

"Okay," I said. "There's a risk. Just like every time we take *The Lost* out to sea. A ship is always safe when it's tied up at the dock, but that's not what ships are built for."

"Did you just make that up?"

"No, I read it somewhere."

"I didn't think you made it up."

"I *told* you I didn't."

"Only because I asked you."

"Well, you only asked because you knew I would tell."

"Of course you would. You're my brother."

"I know."

"Okay."

"We're cool?"

"Totally. You happy?"

I nodded.

"Then finish your Pop-Tart. We need to head over to Fifth Avenue. Where we're all going to die."

Beck was right. Not about the dying part.

It was time for us to suck it up and head over to 983 Fifth Avenue.

So we piled into a taxi and cut across Central Park. Then we stood on the shady sidewalk lining Fifth Avenue, staring up at the towering castle of an apartment building on the other side of the street.

We watched the front door for over an hour. Maybe two.

Storm had brought along a pair of binoculars and pretended she was focused on a hawk roosting behind one of the gargoyles up near the building's roofline.

"The bird is in the nest," she reported when she caught a glimpse of Mr. Aramis moving past

392

a penthouse window. "I repeat: The bird is in the nest."

Finally, at noon, my dive watch's alarm started beeping.

"Here we go," I said.

"Yeah," added Beck. "To our deaths."

"To our deaths!" said Tommy and Storm.

And then we all crossed Fifth Avenue.

CHAPTER 60

Everybody else on Fifth Avenue looked like they belonged on one of the swankiest stretches of real estate anywhere in America.

We did not.

We looked like four tourists on a suicide mission.

Steeling ourselves, we marched up to the door of Mr. Aramis's apartment building. A barrel-chested guy with cauliflower ears and a broken nose, all decked out in a doorman uniform with brass buttons and shoulder boards, blocked our way forward. He looked like one of the guards in *The Wizard of Oz*. If they'd all been ex-boxers.

"May I help youse?" the doorman asked, looking down his flat and crooked nose at us.

"Yes, my good man," I said, because I heard a rich guy say that once when we were docked outside London.

"We need to see Mr. Aramis."

"I'm sorry. Mr. Aramis isn't home."

"Yes, he is," said Storm, tapping the binoculars draped around her neck. "And the lady who lives in the apartment below him needs to buy drapes or a bathrobe."

"Listen, smart mouth," said the doorman, "Mr. Aramis gave me strict orders that he is not to be disturbed this afternoon."

"But that was before he knew we were coming," I said.

"And who, exactly, are *you*?"

"John Keats," I said.

"Who?"

"Just tell Mr. Aramis that we're here with very important information about his most recent art acquisition."

"Really? And exactly which art acquisition might you have been involved with, squirt?"

"The one in Charleston," I said. "The Greek urn he picked up yesterday. Tell Mr. Aramis that his people forgot to take the papers. And, frankly, without the proper paperwork, his new clay pot isn't good for much besides planting petunias. Go ahead, my good man. Make the call."

The doorman had a puzzled, angry look on his face, but he finally called.

And his expression turned to shock. He slowly turned back to us.

"Mr. Aramis says to send youse right up."

CHAPTER 61

The four of us stepped into an elevator that reminded me of a fancy birdcage.

"What floor?" asked an extremely snooty guy

in uniform who, I guessed, sat on a stool all day punching floor numbers for people too rich to punch numbers for themselves.

"The penthouse, if you please," I said, trying to sound as snobby as I could.

"Pleasure," said the elevator operator. He pushed the PH button and cranked a lever, and we whooshed our way up to the twenty-sixth floor.

"My ears just popped," said Tommy, yawning and stretching his jaw. "I hate when that happens. You know what I mean?"

"*Nyes*," said the elevator operator in his clipped British accent. "Indeed."

The car slowed. A bell dinged.

"Penthouse," announced our elevator pilot.

When the shiny doors slid open, we stepped into the Pirate King's palace.

Talk about impressive. The walls were covered with very colorful and very rare paintings—all of them displayed in ornate golden frames, the kind with lots of swirls and curlicues.

"Which one of youse kids is Johnny Keats?"

asked a tough guy with a pistol-shaped bulge under his sport coat.

"Me."

"Who are these other people? More poetical types?"

"No," said Tommy. "We're the Kidds. Dr. Kidd's kids."

"The one what fell off a boat and died?"

"Yeah," I said. "Him."

The guy shook his head. "Tough break. Not for nothin', my dad fell off a boat, too. In Jersey. His shoes were made out of cement at the time. Come on, Keats. You and the Kidds, follow me."

As we crossed the spacious living room, I could hear Storm muttering behind me.

"Renoir. Match. Manet. Match. Monet. Match."

Storm was confirming what I had already suspected: These were the same paintings we'd all seen in the photographs hanging on the walls of The Room.

And I couldn't help but wonder if our dad had helped Mr. Aramis get his grubby hands on them.

CHAPTER 62

T he tough guy escorted us into a wood-paneled library-type room.

Mr. Aramis, his hair slicked back with something thicker than Vaseline, was seated in a high-back leather chair behind a major-league glass desk topped with a fancy pen set and a tiny blue-and-white flag.

"John Keats," Aramis said coldly when we entered his lair, "the renowned English Romantic poet, died in February 1821. Therefore, I am forced to inquire: Who are you irksome little children?"

I think he meant us.

"We're Professor Thomas Kidd's kids," I said.

That's when a guy sitting in a swivel chair in front of the glass desk twirled around to face us.

Nathan Collier.

Apparently, we'd barged in at exactly the right moment. Collier was just now handing our urn over to Aramis.

Collier pulled the wet cigar stub out of his mouth. His face and hands were trembling with rage.

"Didn't I tell you four that the next time we met you would all end up dead?"

"Maybe," I said. "I forget."

"Yeah," said Beck. "When you talk, it's kind of like your TV show. Blah-blah-blah. Bor-ring."

"Why, you little—"

"Silence, Nathan," hissed the Pirate King, raising a delicate hand and twiddling his digits. Collier sat down and did as he was told.

Aramis narrowed his eyes. "So, *children*"—he said the word as if it were a disease—"which one of you had the audacity to tell Bruno downstairs that he was John Keats?"

"That would be me, sir," I said.

"Me, too," said Beck, stepping forward. "We're twins."

"They're really Tom Kidd's kids," Collier blurted out. "He abandoned them at sea right after he

abandoned his quest to find your final treasure for you."

"He didn't abandon anything," said Tommy.

"He just turned the job over to us," added Storm.

"That's right," I said. "Dad took off to go look for that missing Rembrandt. The one he said Mr. Aramis might enjoy adding to his collection."

"Ha!" said Collier. "What 'missing' Rembrandt?"

"*Storm on the Sea of Galilee*," said Storm.

Mr. Aramis leaned forward over his glass-topped desk. We had his attention. "Fascinating," he said. "Your father knew where to find that particular Rembrandt?"

"Yep," I said. "Just like he knew where to find that." I gestured toward the Grecian urn. "See, unlike some treasure hunters, our dad actually delivers the goods."

"Including the documents proving that a treasure is, you know, *a treasure*," said Beck, whipping out the provenance papers.

Aramis scowled at Collier. "You told me there was no historical documentation attached to this object, Nathan."

"There wasn't. Not in the gym bag. There was nothing in there but a smelly sweatshirt."

"That's right," I said. "Because every halfway decent treasure hunter knows you never keep the papers with the prize."

"Makes things too easy for lazy thieves and pilfering pirates," added Beck, kind of hissing the words at Collier.

"Yo," said the thug with the gun bulge on his chest. "Watch your language. Mr. Aramis here is the Pirate King."

"Sorry, sir," said Beck. "No disrespect."

"You will be forgiven," said Aramis with a sickly smile, "as soon as you hand over those papers." He extended his bony fingers in Beck's general direction.

"And why, exactly, would I want to do that?"

"So he doesn't rip out your fingernails with a pair of pliers!" shouted Collier.

"Nathan?" said Mr. Aramis, shaking his head and putting a finger to his lips to silence his yapping lapdog.

"Sorry, sir," said Collier. "Won't happen again."

"See that it doesn't." Aramis focused his coal-black eyes on Beck. "Young lady, after I study those provenance papers and feel confident that I am in possession of the genuine Grecian urn immortalized by the *real* John Keats, I will complete the transaction with my clients in Cyprus."

"The thugs who took our mother?" said Tommy.

"The very same," said Mr. Aramis. "Who knows? Once I release their arms shipment, perhaps those angry young men will finally set your mother free. Now, then, kindly hand me those papers."

The tough guy who had escorted us into the room reached under his bulging sport coat and pulled out...a wad of Kleenex.

"Sorry, boss," he said, blowing his nose. "It's all these dusty antiques and picture frames. Allergies."

The goon didn't have a gun.

I glanced at Beck.

She gave me the slightest nod.

"Wait a second!" I shouted. "Our father did not work for you, and he is not dead."

"Actually, Bick, Dad is dead."

"No, he is not!"

Beck smiled at Mr. Aramis. "Please forgive my brother. Sometimes he loses touch with reality."

"I do not!"

"Yes, you do!"

And, just like we planned, we launched into Twin Tirade No. 434.

CHAPTER 63

"**D**ad is not dead, Rebecca!" I shouted.

"He is too, Bickford."

"No, he's not!"

"That's enough," said Mr. Aramis. "Silence, please. Your voices grate on my nerves."

So Beck and I amped up our rant.

"Whose side are you on, Rebecca?"

"Yours, Bickford. But I'm just telling the truth."

"Then how come you keep saying Dad is dead?"

"Because he *is*!"

"No, he's not!"

Aramis tried again. "Silence! Now!"

We weren't listening. "Then where is he?" said
Beck.

"On a top secret treasure hunt!"

"What?"

"A helicopter picked him up."

"Nathan?" Aramis's face was turning purple.
"Do something. Make these children cease this
senseless bickering!"

"Shut up, kids!" shouted Collier.

Beck ignored him. "Ha! A helicopter?"

"Yeah. They snatched him off the deck with a rescue rope."

"Really? In the middle of a hurricane?"

"Mr. Collier?" said Aramis, rubbing his eyes with both hands like he had a migraine headache. "Do something! Now! Or you will be relieved of your duties!"

"Okay, you little brats," snapped Collier. "Knock it off!"

Beck and I kept going. "A very noisy hurricane so we couldn't hear the propellers!"

"That's impossible!"

"Nuh-uh. Not if the helicopter pilot was really, really good."

"You, Bick, are completely whacked."

"And you, Beck, are extremely dumb."

"Take that back!"

"I will if you say Dad isn't dead."

"He *is*!"

"Is *not*!"

"Is too!"

"Says who?"

412

"*Me!*"

"*Ha!*"

"*Ha* yourself!"

"*Silence!*" screamed Mr. Aramis as he leaped up so ferociously it sent his chair flying backward into a bookshelf. Fuming, just like Beck and I figured he would, he grabbed his gold-plated pistol and aimed it at us. "I cannot abide screaming children, crying babies, or barking dogs! If the two of you don't stop this tirade by the time I count to three, I will most definitely give you something to scream about."

Beck and I quickly glanced around the room. Aramis was the only one waggling a weapon. So far, our plan was working perfectly.

"One!" said Aramis.

I took a deep breath. Glowered hard at Beck.

"Dad. Is. Not. Dead!"

Beck glowered hard at me. "Yes. He. Is!"

"Two!" shouted Aramis, raising his pistol, swinging it back and forth, trying to decide which one of us to shoot first.

He was about to say "Three!" when Tommy sprang into action and leaped at Aramis with a flying karate kick.

CHAPTER 64

Tommy's left foot slammed into Aramis's wrist.

It made a sound like a snapping chicken bone. The pistol went flying.

Storm grabbed Collier, yanking him up by the shirt.

"This is for the stupid little map you had stupid Louie Louie stuff in the stupid bee pendant! You made me cry. I'm Storm Kidd. I don't do tears." Then, flipping through her photographic memory to the spot where the pre-med student attacked Tommy, Storm kneed Collier where it really, really hurt.

"Ooof!" cried Collier, his eyes watering up with pain.

"Look who's crying now!" Storm gloated.

Beck held the bodyguard with the runny nose at bay by striking an arms-up attack pose.

When Tommy grabbed Aramis's gun off the floor, I lunged for the Grecian urn.

Unfortunately, Aramis did the exact same thing.

Together, we tipped the ancient vase off the edge of the glass-topped table.

"Noooo!" shouted Aramis.

The urn was tumbling toward the floor.

I shot out my arms and snagged it. The instant I had it in my hands, I flipped my body so I'd land with my butt on the ground instead of a vase in my face.

"Got it!" I shouted as I lay on the ground, the priceless treasure nestled against my chest.

"Good," sneered Aramis. "Now hand it over."

I looked up.

In all the commotion, six more bodyguards had tromped into the room.

These six were not blowing their noses.

They were all aiming their weapons straight down at me.

So much for heroics.

Beck had been right: We were all going to die.

CHAPTER 65

"Kill them!" shouted Aramis. "Kill them all! But whatever you do, don't you dare hurt my new urn!"

Three of the goons aimed their guns at my head. The other three swung around to train their weapons on Beck, Storm, and Tommy.

"So," I said, "I guess this means you don't want that Rembrandt?"

"I'll find it for you!" said Collier. "I'm very good at what I do."

"Ha!" snorted Beck. "In your dreams."

Aramis motioned for his men to wait a moment before executing us. He leaned over to quiz me.

"Do you really know where to find this priceless Rembrandt, young man?"

"Of course we do," I said. "We're real treasure hunters. Not phonies like certain people named, oh, *Collier*."

"Don't listen to them," said Nathan Collier. "I can find it."

"No, you can't," said Beck.

"Yes, I can."

"Cannot."

"Can too!"

Just as they were about to erupt into their own tirade, I finally heard a hubbub out in the hallway. The one that was supposed to happen, like, five minutes earlier.

Doors banged. Gruff voices shouted. A squadron of feet marched across the living room.

Then I heard another very loud *BANG* followed by a ringing *PA-PING*!

A gunshot.

"What's going on?" demanded Aramis.

One of the gun-toting goons grabbed Storm to use her as a human shield.

Big mistake.

She elbowed him in the gut while she kicked another of the thugs in what we'll call his "Collier."

Tommy took out three of the other guys with karate chops that could split bricks. Beck took down another by spin-kicking his ankles out from under him. He collided with the last goon, bringing them both to the floor.

The door to the study burst open.

"Drop your weapons!" shouted a familiar voice.

And then I saw the familiar mirrored sunglasses.

Uncle Timothy had brought along about twenty friends, all of them with serious weaponry and flak jackets that had FBI and CIA in big, bold letters plastered on their fronts and backs.

The bad guys, already in excruciating pain from sparring with my sibs, were smart enough to see that they were seriously outnumbered *and* outgunned. They immediately dropped their weapons and raised their hands.

"Hi, kids," said Uncle Timothy. "Sorry we're a little late."

"You guys were supposed to be here, like, five minutes ago!" said Beck.

"It's all my fault," said Dr. Lewis, toddling into the room. "I misplaced the napkin where I had jotted down the address you gave me last night."

"Okay, Aramis," said Uncle Timothy. "The game is over. You're coming with us."

I gave the Grecian urn to Dr. Lewis, figuring he'd know how to handle it, since he was a professor of Old Stuff That Breaks Easily.

"Kindly return that item," said Aramis when he saw me hand off the ancient artifact. "It belongs to me."

"Really?" said Uncle Timothy. "How much a planter like that run you?"

Aramis was smirking again. "More than you'll ever make during your entire career, Officer."

"It's priceless!" added Collier. He dusted off his bomber jacket, trying to act like he was somebody important. "Officers, I am an expert on these matters, and I assure you, a treasure such as this one is worth one million, maybe two million dollars."

Uncle Timothy whistled like he was impressed. Then he jabbed a thumb over his shoulder. "And all those paintings in the other room? What are they worth?"

"Oh, I wouldn't want to tax your feeble little brain with that information," gloated Aramis. "The figures are astronomically high."

"I see," said Uncle Timothy. "Mike? Could you step in here for a minute?"

A mild-mannered man wearing thick glasses stepped into the room.

"This is Michael Stewart," said Uncle Timothy. "He works for the IRS."

Mr. Aramis and Nathan Collier looked confused, so Uncle Timothy explained.

"You know, the Internal Revenue Service. The tax people?"

"I know what the IRS is," bellowed Aramis. "But why is this man here in my home?"

It was Uncle Timothy's turn to smirk. "I think he wants to tax your gigantic brain, sir."

"Quick question, if you don't mind, Mr. Aramis," said IRS Agent Stewart, clicking one of his pens as he pulled a file folder out of his briefcase. "How were you able to afford all this artwork?"

"What do you mean?"

Athos Aramis—whose name sure sounded like it might be Greek—might have been confused, but I wasn't. The last piece of my dad's puzzle had just clicked into place. I turned to Beck with a smirk on my face.

"How much does a Grecian earn?" we recited in unison.

The IRS agent smiled. "Apparently not very much. We noticed, Mr. Aramis, that last year you didn't pay any income tax at all, because, according to your tax return, you didn't have a job, let alone any W-2s."

Professor Lewis chuckled. "Oh, ho. No job. Very funny. Very funny, indeed."

"Was that intended to be a joke?" said Mr.

Aramis. "If so, I fail to see the humor in it."

"Then allow me to explain," said Uncle Timothy. "Athos Aramis?"

"Yes?"

"You are under arrest."

"Oh, really? For what?"

"Income tax evasion."

CHAPTER 66

As you probably already figured out, Beck and I had set up the little raid with the help of Dr. Lewis after we "looked at the big picture" and figured out that Mom and Dad had been working as double agents.

They'd only been *pretending* to work for Mr. Aramis so they could help the CIA, FBI, and IRS build their case against the notorious arms dealer. They needed evidence that would guarantee that the Pirate King would go to jail, no matter how many powerful, well-connected friends he had.

Unfortunately, Mr. Aramis was excellent at covering his tracks and hiding any paperwork that could send him to jail for illegal arms dealing. So, the CIA decided to go with Operation Al Capone.

Yep. That's why Dad had the notorious Chicago gangster's newspaper clipping pinned up on the board alongside all the photographs of Mr. Aramis's art in The Room.

Back in 1931, Al Capone went to jail, not because he'd been running rum, smuggling stuff, and rubbing people out on a regular basis. He went to jail for—drumroll, please—*income tax evasion.*

Athos Aramis was about to do the same thing.

Because, as the IRS agent pointed out, how could he own all the wildly expensive art on display in his stunning penthouse apartment if he had zero income, which is what he'd reported on his tax return?

As the FBI guys slapped handcuffs on Aramis and read him his rights, I could see Beck, Tommy, and Storm all breathe a sigh of relief.

This thing was over.

The four of us had, without too much adult supervision, just completed Dad's supersecret, undercover mission.

Or had we?

"Wait a second!" I said. "What about Mom?"

CHAPTER 67

"The young man is absolutely right," said Aramis, still smiling smugly, even though his hands were tied behind his back. "You can, of course, arrest me on this silly, trumped-up tax charge. But if you do, rest assured these four will never, ever see their mother alive again."

There's always a hitch, isn't there? I hate it when that happens.

"Her only hope rests with me authorizing the release of certain *merchandise* to some very angry, very violent young men over in Cyprus,"

Aramis went on. "Something, I must say, I would not feel inclined to do if I find myself trading in my custom-tailored Italian suit for a bright orange prison jumpsuit."

The room went completely silent.

Nobody said a word.

We all looked to Uncle Timothy. After all, he was Mom's handler—her boss at the CIA. If Mr. Aramis didn't make the phone call to release the weapons, Beck and I would never have to do another Twin Tirade about Mom's fate.

Because she'd definitely be dead.

On the other hand, we didn't do everything Dad would have done to put Mr. Aramis behind bars just to hand him a Get Out of Jail Free card at the end of the game.

Uncle Timothy stayed silent for what seemed like forever.

Then, finally, he reached into one of his pockets and pulled out a slim satellite phone that looked like the kind Martians probably use.

He handed it to Aramis.

"Make the call," he said.

EPILOGUE

CHAPTER 68

We sailed south from New York to North Carolina and used some of our college fund to rent a funky beach house right on the water.

We docked *The Lost* in a very nice marina where she'd get her a fresh coat of paint and be prepped for our next adventure.

Oh, by the way, our college fund recently registered a brand-new five-hundred-thousand-dollar deposit because we'd picked up a half-million-dollar reward for finding all the stolen art up in Mr. Aramis's penthouse.

Aramis had cut a deal to stay out of jail. But

no way were the FBI, CIA, or the IRS going to let him keep all those art treasures.

Tommy is already getting along famously with the North Carolina locals, including a girl named Kara Kerz.

Don't worry.

Storm did a very thorough background check once we lifted her fingerprints off a Snapple bottle. Kara Kerz is not a pirate *or* a surfer chick.

Meanwhile, Uncle Timothy and his team at the CIA are hot on the Mom trail over in Cyprus. Apparently, the Agency was more interested in tracking down the Cypriot terrorists than busting Aramis. The whole double-agent thing was part of another, even bigger sting operation. They *wanted* Aramis to make that satellite phone call just so they could track the weapons' movements.

(When your mother and father both work for the CIA, your whole life is like the inside of a kaleidoscope. There's no way for you to ever tell which way is up.)

Anyway, Uncle Timothy has a "high degree of confidence" that his team will not only take down the terrorists but also find Mom. So now even Beck is optimistic. We might get the good news about a successful "Momma Bear" rescue any day.

And Dad? Well, I still think he's alive. Somewhere. Probably on a super secret mission for the CIA, the kind nobody can talk about. The kind the government would deny ever existed if the mission didn't end the way it was supposed to.

So while the four of us wait for our parents to come home to *The Lost*, we'll keep the family business running. We'll hunt for the other treasures on Dad's to-do list. We're in a little bit of a hurry because we want to find every single one before Nathan Collier gets lucky and accidentally stumbles across any of them.

That's right. The FBI took Collier into custody and questioned him. But there was no solid evidence to connect him to any of the stolen art in Aramis's lair. Uncle Timothy did, however, make sure that Collier bought Tommy a new gym bag and replaced his sweatshirt.

"We need to head back out to sea," said Beck as we sat on the porch of our beach house watching

Tommy flirt with his new friend and Storm build a sand castle that looked exactly like the Taj Mahal.

"Definitely," I said.

"Soon."

"Really soon."

"Like tomorrow."

"Tomorrow would be awesome."

Yep. There would be no Twin Tirade about it. The treasure-hunting life is in our blood. Chasing after the next adventure out there, whatever it might be, was just how we Wild Things had to live.

CHAPTER 69

"You guys?" Beck was on the front porch of our North Carolina beach house blasting an air horn.

WHOMP! WHOMP! WHOMP! WHOMP! WHOMP!

Everybody came running. It's still Kidd Family Rule No. 1. A triple blast always means somebody's in trouble and needs help. So a fourth and fifth blast was off-the-charts freaky....

Then Beck blasted out an unheard-of *sixth WHOMP!*

"What's *up*?" said Tommy as he came running up the beach.

Storm had slammed through the screen door, twirling her nunchucks.

I'd raced up the walkway at the side of the house because I had been a block away, down on Main Street, where there was a cool Internet café.

"We just got an e-mail!" shouted Beck, waving a sheet of printer paper. "From Dad!"

"No way," said Tommy.

"You're kidding!" I cried.

"Is it real?" asked Storm.

"Definitely. Who else would know this?" Beck said, and read the e-mail:

I suggest you four now go after a treasure trove near the top of my list: King Solomon's Mines. Go to Africa and find my friend Dumaka. I hope to join you there but must first complete my current job for Uncle T. I'm sorry I had to take off like that in the storm. But when the helicopter showed up and the pilot relayed my new mission, I had no choice. I had to follow orders.

The LOST

Beck looked at me. "You were right!"

"I knew it was a helicopter!" I exclaimed. "Just like that one that picked up Uncle Timothy."

"Awesome," said Tommy. "I want to do that someday. Have a helicopter hoist me up. In a hurricane, too!"

Storm rolled her eyes. "En-joy, Tommy. En-joy."

"What else does he say?" I asked.

"That he loves us dearly and that the next time we're all together he'll explain everything. Well, everything he can explain without getting into trouble with the Agency."

Beck sounded a little choked up when she read us how Dad had wrapped up his e-mail:

I could not be happier with you, my four wonderful Wild Things. You completed my mission. You made me proud to be your father. You saved your mother's life. You are the best children any father could ever hope for. With great love, faithfully, your dad.

PS—Trust Uncle Timothy, but never, ever with your lives.

PPS—Rebecca, it's time to put away the 3-D glasses. They've served their purpose. Your mom doesn't find them becoming. I do, but I've been outvoted.

CHAPTER 70

S o, sometime next week, we'll be setting sail for Africa.

King Solomon's mythical mines, filled with diamonds and gold, are real and just waiting for us to excavate their treasure. Dad and Mom might join us on the hunt.

If the CIA can follow through on its plans to rescue Mom.

And if Dad really is alive.

That e-mail Beck read? I wrote it. Uncle Timothy had talked me through how to send it from the nearby Internet café so it'd look a lot more legitimate than that fake e-mail Beck had tried to fool the cop with when we were fleeing the Cayman Islands.

Hey, I warned you not to believe everything you read.

Of course, that doesn't mean it isn't true.

Because, deep in my heart, I really do think Dad and Mom are still alive. In fact, they're the two treasures at the top of *my* treasure-hunting list.

Beck's, too.

How can I be so sure?

Easy.

It's a twin thing.

FLOP SWEAT

Have you ever done something extremely stupid like, oh, I don't know, try to make a room filled with total strangers laugh until their sides hurt?

Totally dumb, right?

Well, that's why my humble story is going to start with some pretty yucky tension—plus a little heavy-duty drama (and, hopefully, a few funnies so we don't all go nuts).

Okay, so how, exactly, did I get into this mess—up onstage at a comedy club, baking like a bag of French fries under a hot spotlight that shows off my sweat stains (including one that sort of looks like Jabba the Hutt), with about a thousand beady eyeballs drilling into me?

A very good question that you ask.

To tell you the truth, it's one *I'm* asking, too!

What am I, Jamie Grimm, doing here trying to win something called the Planet's Funniest Kid Comic Contest?

What was I thinking?

But wait. Hold on. It gets even worse.

While the whole audience stares and waits for me to say something (anything) funny, I'm up here choking.

That's right—my mind is a *total and complete blank*.

And I just said, "No, I'm Jamie Grimm."

That's the punch line. The *end* of a joke.

All it needs is whatever comes *before* the punch line. You know—all the stuff *I can't remember*.

So I sweat some more. The audience stares some more.

I don't think this is how a comedy act is supposed to go. I'm pretty sure *jokes* are usually involved. And people laughing.

"Um, hi." I finally squeak out a few words. "The other day at school, we had this substitute teacher.

Very tough. Sort of like Mrs. Darth Vader. Had the heavy breathing, the deep voice. During roll call, she said, 'Are you chewing gum, young man?' And I said, 'No, I'm Jamie Grimm.'"

I wait (for what seems like hours) and, yes, the audience kind of chuckles. It's not a huge laugh, but it's a start.

Okay. *Phew*. I can tell a joke. All is not lost. Yet. But hold on for a sec. We need to talk about something else. A major twist to my tale.

"A major twist?" you say. "Already?"

Yep. And, trust me, you weren't expecting this one.

To be totally honest, neither was I.

LADIES AND GENTLEMEN...ME!

Hi.

Presenting me. Jamie Grimm. The sit-down comic.

So, can you deal with this? Some people can. Some can't. Sometimes even *I* can't deal with it (like just about every morning, when I wake up and look at myself in the mirror).

But you know what they say: "If life gives you lemons, learn how to juggle."

Or, even better, learn how to make people laugh.

So that's what I decided to do.

Seriously. I tried to teach myself how to be funny. I did a whole bunch of homework and read every joke book and joke website I could find, just so I could become a comedian and make people laugh.

I guess you could say I'm obsessed with being a stand-up comic—even though I don't exactly fit the job description.

But unlike a lot of homework (algebra, you know I'm talking about *you*), this was fun.

I got to study all the greats: Jon Stewart, Jerry Seinfeld, Kevin James, Ellen DeGeneres, Chris Rock, Steven Wright, Joan Rivers, George Carlin.

I also filled dozens of notebooks with jokes I made up myself—like my second one-liner at the comedy contest.

"Wow, what a crowd," I say, surveying the audience. "Standing room only. Good thing I brought my own chair."

It takes a second, but they laugh—right after I let them know it's okay, because *I'm* smiling, too.

This second laugh? Well, it's definitely bigger than that first chuckle. Who knows—maybe I actually have a shot at winning this thing.

So now I'm not only nervous, I'm *pumped*!

I really, really, *really* (and I mean really) want to take my best shot at becoming the Planet's Funniest Kid Comic.

Because, in a lot of ways, my whole life has been leading up to this one sweet (if sweaty) moment in the spotlight!

A day without sunshine is like, you know, night.

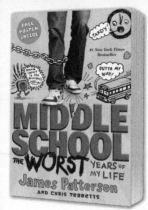

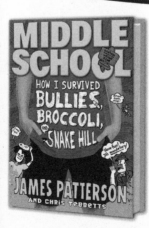

JAMES PATTERSON was selected by readers across America as the Children's Choice Book Awards Author of the Year in 2010. He is the internationally bestselling author of the highly praised Middle School books, *I Funny*, *Confessions of a Murder Suspect*, and the Maximum Ride, Witch & Wizard, Daniel X, and Alex Cross series. His books have sold more than 275 million copies worldwide, making him one of the bestselling authors of all time. He lives in Florida.

CHRIS GRABENSTEIN is a *New York Times* bestselling author who has also collaborated with James Patterson on the I Funny series and *Daniel X: Armageddon*. He lives in New York City.

JULIANA NEUFELD is an award-winning illustrator whose drawings can be found in books, on album covers, and in nooks and crannies throughout the Internet. She lives in Toronto.